ART FOR ALL SEASONS

Susan Schwake

PHOTOGRAPHY
Rainer Schwake

KIDS ART SERIES

ART FOR ALL SEASONS

40 CREATIVE MIXED MEDIA ADVENTURES FOR CHILDREN - INSPIRED BY NATURE AND CONTEMPORARY ARTISTS

Susan Schwake

Photography
Layout and Design
Rainer Schwake

twolittlebirdsbooks.com

Acknowledgments

Egbert –
Vielen Dank!
Cheerio, my old friend!

Rebecca –
Without your vision and clarity this book would not have been possible. Thank you for your friendship and hard work!

Rainer –
What partnership works overtime 24/7? Our love does, clearly.

Grace –
Your diligence and attention to detail is second to none. So proud of you, love!

Chloe –
Your creativity inspires me daily – thank you, love!

Contents

Introduction 11
Art Materials List 15
Art-Making Space 19

Spring 20
Happy Scrappy Flowers 22
Raindrop Shapes 24
Umbrella Shapes 26
Spring Relief Painting 28
Garden Tile 30
May Baskets 32
Relief Printed Cards 36
Pysanky Eggs 40
Bugs! 42
Wrapped Vase 44

Summer 48
Feather Paintings 50
Relief Sand Castings 52
Record Mandala 54
Sun Prints 56
Breezy Wind Chimes 58
Summer Abstract Painting 60
Bubble Fish Mobile 62
Drawing Nature 66
Painting Outside 70
Button Fish 72

Autumn 74
Clay Totem Poles 76
Place Cards 78
Woodland Mask 80
Leaf Patterns 84
Stitched Family Portraits 86
Nature Journals 90
Fall Shadow Box 92
Animal Forms 94
Printed Napkins 96
Leaf Table Runner 98

Winter 102
Cozy Animals 104
Salt Clay Ornaments 108
Snowy Prints 110
Mini Art Accordion Books 114
Paper Trees 118
Paper Quilts 122
Winter Animal Banner 126
Tin Can Tracks 130
Forest Plaster Cottage 132
Winter Night Drawing 136

Recipes 138
Resources 141
Contributors 142
About the Author 144

Introduction

We walk in the woods, play in the snow, splash in the waves and nurture seedlings each year. Here in New England, we herald the seasons with fanfare, as often the changes are long awaited. There is much to inspire us within these changes – shapes, color, texture, mood, light and drama. With a sense of wonder – of exploration – these lessons guide you to look to the natural world for inspiration.

This book was written to inspire the teacher, parent, child care provider, grandparent and anyone wanting to make art with (and possibly alongside) a child. The focus of these lessons is to take a little time exploring nature as well as the art process and combine the experiences to a creative outcome. It is always about the process in our studio and enjoying the process deeply.

For children, art is a way to convey their experiences and feelings about the world. It helps them define and evaluate their world. Sometimes art making doesn't go as planned and the end product doesn't work out as envisioned – that's okay. It takes a lot of practice! These lessons are designed to repeat over and over to gain competency through repetition, expand creative thought and increase the maker's skill set.

I have found as a teacher of both children and adults that everyone learns through practice. I encourage students of all ages to try the same lesson twice at the very least and letting newfound knowledge guide their process. I encourage you, the adult, to work alongside the students to discover the joy of the process for yourself. Investigate your creativity again and help explain, without words, your world.

Introduction

The Art Materials List is a guide to often-used materials and a simple "art studio" setup. It is a comprehensive list for all of the lessons in the book, but you don't need all the materials for each lesson. Each lesson outlines the materials that are needed to create the project and gives options for expansion on the lesson. Many of the materials on the list are from nature itself. Remember to respect nature when collecting specimens.

I encourage you to set up an area to exhibit and celebrate the work that is made. This elevates the process to a place to be admired and remembered. A simple string with clothespins to hang flat work can fit in the tiniest of spaces. A shelf or table below can hold sculptural work. For larger rooms, a cork strip or wire curtain rod can run along a wall to hold a classroom full of artwork. It is important to celebrate the creative process without making it all too precious. I often have parents lament about where to display or how to keep artwork in their homes. One of the easiest ways to hold on to the work is to photograph it and have a simple photo book made. We found this to be a great solution for many families. We also gave special pieces to relatives who would appreciate the artwork. Another way to display work is to have a Lucite box frame arrangement on the wall of various standard sizes, ready to display the latest work. Sometimes I have asked my own children if they have art that they would like to recycle into bookmarks or greeting cards. This has been a fun way to enjoy the initial artwork once again by making something new and by spreading the love to friends. At the end of each year, in our home, I went through the art that was made and kept one piece for myself and one for each child. These pieces went into paper portfolios and we often pull them out for a look. The rest gets photographed and the originals recycled.

Many of the lessons in this book can be adapted from season to season. I think of them as springboards for your own interpretation. There are many ways that each of these lessons can be done – be open and let your personal expression flow freely! In a classroom setting, there can be as many outcomes to each lesson as there are students. Most of all, enjoy the process of the lessons. Embrace the differences and then admire the results!

It is my greatest hope that these lessons inspire art making and a closer look at the natural world around us.

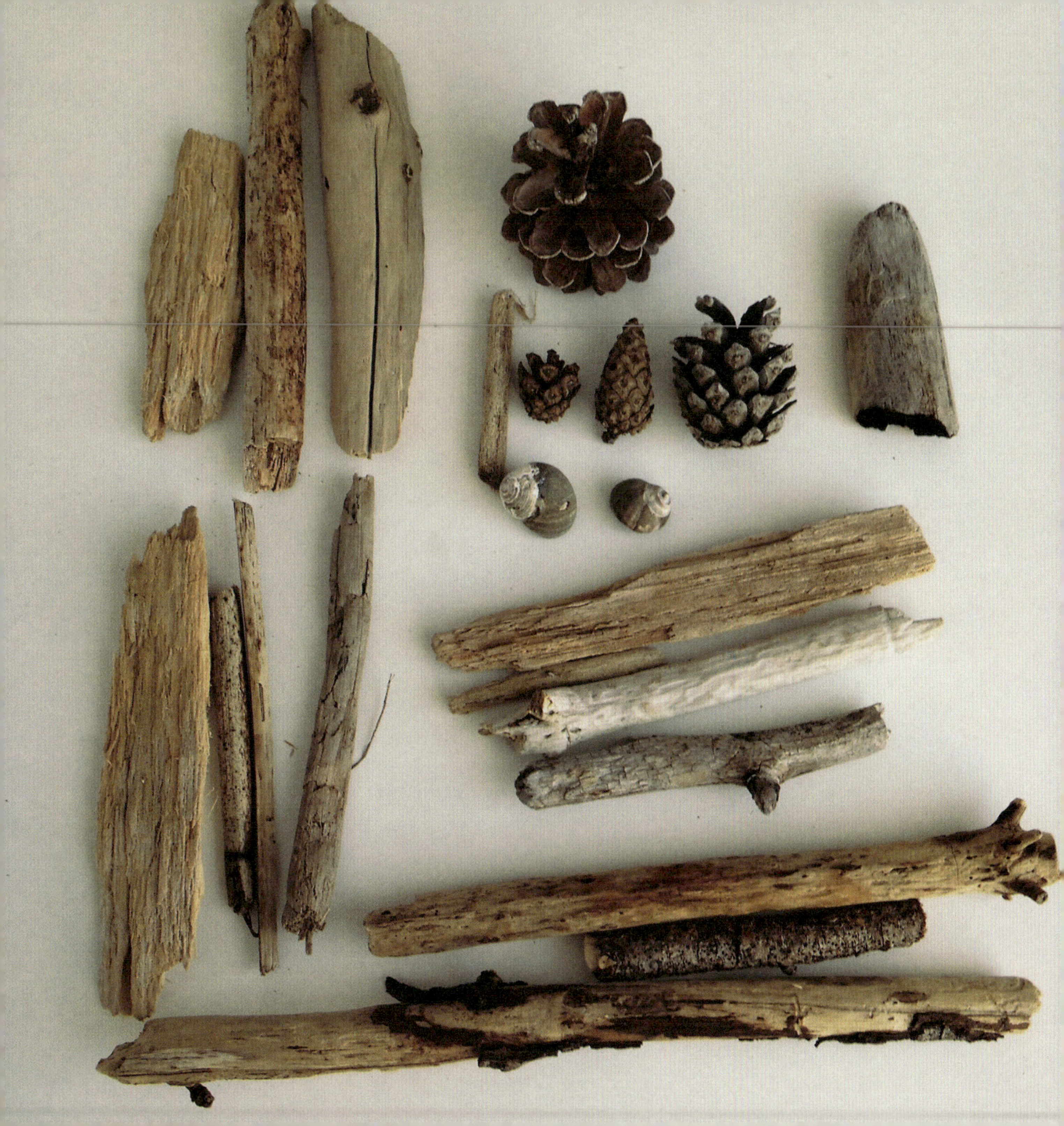

PRIMARY ARTIST
PRIMARY ARTIST
12 REEVES BRISTLE HAIR
10 Flat
Artist's Loft
12 REEVES BRISTLE HAIR
8 BLICK SCHOLASTIC OX HAIR
BRIGHT
6 REEVES BRISTLE HAIR

Art Materials List

The following is a list of items that will help build your art making space. From simple furnishings to basic materials, this list will get you started. Collecting these supplies over time is easiest and most cost effective, however, many of these items you may already have on hand. Don't be daunted by the list – just collect as you can and once people know you are collecting, they will be keeping special items for you! Keep them in labeled boxes on shelves for easy storage or in open bins in a corner for easy access. Our studio has a combination of pull out clear drawers and shelves for items we use often and trays and bins for specialty supplies.

MATERIALS

- Newspapers and plastic tablecloths for drop cloths.
- Paper plates, Plexiglas, wax paper or a cookie sheet for a paint palette.
- Plastic wrap, wax paper and aluminum foil.
- Found objects such as: bottle caps, buttons, fabric scraps, small boxes, corks, plastics of all sorts, shells, pebbles, tiny toys, ribbon, etc., sorted into labeled bags or jars.
- From the toolbox: screwdriver, nails, hammer, washers, sandpaper, foam brushes.
- From the kitchen drawer: liquid soap, wooden spoons, sponges, straws, cookie sheets, rags, clean recycled foam trays from the grocery store, netted bags from produce, clean plastic containers, and plastic cutlery.

Art Materials List

- Papers of all sorts: mat board, foam core, old artwork, discarded books, colored papers, tissue paper, magazines, old safety envelopes, junk mail, sheet music, catalogs, other interesting recycled papers.
- Adhesives: white glue, Tacky Glue, clear glue, glue sticks (UHU is my favorite) , contact cement, hot glue, and wood glue are all handy to have.
- When gluing paper, we recommend UHU glue sticks. They work well and last long. White glue is great for lightweight materials such as feathers and yarn. Tacky Glue is what we use to glue on pebbles and button-weight materials. Hot glue is for fast tacking or when we can't wait for something to dry. E6000 is for really heavy items such as clay pieces and should be used by an adult.
- Spray clear coat for use outside by an adult.
- Canvas boards, canvas, plywood, Masonite, found wood and fiberboard – all primed with acrylic gesso for painting on. Or prime with house paint that is leftover.

- Oil pastels, crayons, watercolor pans, acrylic paint, paint markers, glaze for ceramics, graphite pencils, colored pencils, tempera paint and colorful permanent markers and gel pens for color. Buy the best you can afford. Liquid watercolors are nice, too.
- Found nature items are part of this book's lessons. Please remember not to pick flowers that are endangered or not yours, or strip bark from live trees. Do search the ground for leaves, acorns, twigs, rocks, shells and other bits of nature that are inspiring to you. If you do not use them in the project – return them to the earth!

- Brushes of all sorts: foam, bristle, nylon, and foam brayers, hard and soft brayers for printmaking.
- Scissors, hole punches and craft knives (to be used by or with an adult).
- Oven-bake clay comes in many brands. It is a pliable clay that doesn't dry out and can be hardened by baking it according to directions on the package in your own kitchen oven. We use Sculpy with great success.
- When using stoneware clay, salt clay and oven-bake clays in this book, a few tools will be helpful: toothpicks, pin tool, scoring tools (we made ours – as shown below – with a paint stirrer, pins and epoxy via Megan Bogonovich's brilliant idea!), clay sponges, doilies, wooden rolling pin, wooden slats for guides, canvas cloth to work on, kiln or access to one, oven, stamps, plastic bags, small bowls for water and E6000 glue for repairing broken work.
- Clay used in this book is low-fire cone 04 white. For color we use underglazes and a protective clear glaze in the final firing to make the pieces food-safe. We also use plasticine clay, Sculpy brand oven-bake clay and salt dough clay (recipe is in the back of the book).

Art-Making Space

Having a dedicated studio is a luxury that many students do not have. It is simple, however, to make a small studio most anywhere that can facilitate great art-making! Here are a few suggestions for making a comfortable art making area where creativity can run wild.

- Find an area where a surface can be cleared for working. This surface should be equipped with a chair that is the proper height for the student (feet on the floor and waist-high surface top). The area does not have to be large or permanent. A folding table will do!
- There should be plenty of light from windows or lamps or both.
- Cover the surface with either newspaper or a plastic tablecloth.
- If the floor below the table is not easily cleaned, you can cover that as well with a tarp or plastic table cloth.
- Have an apron or old t-shirt handy for each artist.
- Store your materials in bins, on trays, or in jars on nearby shelves if you have them. If shelves are not available, a large box or basket can store away materials and yet be handy to pull out when needed. I love using trays! I use them to organize my supplies on my shelves and to bring the specific materials I need for a lesson to the work area.
- A source for water – a sink is ideal, but a bucket of clean water and a bucket for wastewater works well!

SPRING

SPRING

Spring brings so much joy to us, here in New England. Its long awaited arrival makes us marvel at the first bud we see. Even the rain is a happy sight, as our gardens are waiting for water and everything outside wants winter washed away. It is a time when spending time drawing and observing nature without a jacket can be done again.

Finding a nest filled with blue eggs or some baby birds is a treat for the springtime explorer. It is a time when the seeds that you planted become tiny versions of what they will grow to. The earth smells washed and clean and is filling up with the color green. There are many gifts that spring gives us that can inspire us to create something from.

Happy Scrappy Flowers

MATERIALS

- Fresh flowers
- Scissors
- Assorted colored papers
- Glue Stick for paper
- Background paper
- Assorted buttons
- Clear glue for buttons

INSPIRED BY ALBINA MCPHAIL

For Albina, painting is an exploration, a journey of stepping away from the familiar only to find it again, in however unlikely a form or abstraction.

Connect *by Albina McPhail*

GET READY!

Cutting paper and gluing shapes to make a painting is called collage. It is a fun way to use up scrap paper and recycle old envelopes, sheet music and magazines. Springtime brings flowers and their diverse petal shapes are fun to study and cut from paper. If you don't have any fresh flowering plants on hand look at some botanical books at the library or seed catalogs. Silk flowers are a great reference source too.

LET'S MAKE ART!

1. Choose your papers by color, texture and size to make the stems, petals, leaves and grass or vase.
2. Cut out the petals, stems and leaves of each flower.
3. To create layered petals, stack the cut paper petals.
4. Tearing the paper gives a different edge for the petals or leaves
5. Arrange your flowers and glue them down.
6. Add button centers if desired.

EXPLORE MORE

Try making a forest of trees with cut paper collage. Collage a bouquet on a greeting card!

Raindrop Shapes

MATERIALS

- Set of watercolor pans
- Soft watercolor brush
- Watercolor paper
- Water container
- Newspaper

INSPIRED BY HEATHER SMITH JONES

Heather Smith Jones, MFA, is an artist working in painting, drawing, photography, and printmaking. She is an instructor at an arts-based preschool and the author of *Water Paper Paint, Exploring Creativity with Watercolor and Mixed Media.* Smith Jones lives in Lawrence, KS with her husband and their four felines.

All Things New *by Heather Smith Jones*

GET READY!

Sitting at a window watching the Spring rain fall in droplets is a fascinating way to pass the time. Each drop is formed in the air and when it hits the ground the shape changes completely. You can capture this experience with a watercolor brush and watercolor paints on paper to "save for a sunny day."

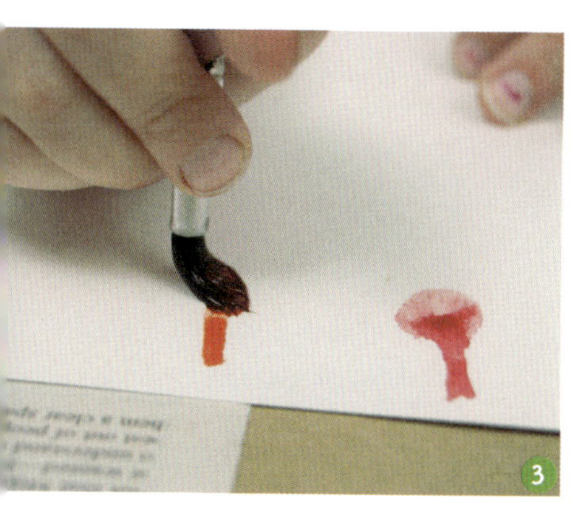

LET'S MAKE ART!

1. Start with a wet brush and your favorite color of paint.
2. Lightly touch the paper with the tip of the brush.
3. Press down with the brush to create a droplet while pulling it slightly towards you.
4. Change colors and make more droplets in a pattern of your choice.
5. Fill the entire paper with colorful droplets.

EXPLORE MORE

Try cutting your paper into one large droplet shape and glue it onto another paper. Make a rainy day painting filling the sky with raindrops.

Umbrella Shapes

GET READY!

Umbrellas are a common sight in springtime, bobbing up and down a busy sidewalk. This half circle shape is a great shape for studying negative spaces and overlapping shapes.

MATERIALS

- Cover stock
- Chalk pastels
- Colored paper
- Plastic round container
- Pencils
- Glue stick
- Dark colored background paper
- Fixative

INSPIRED BY JENNIFER SKOROPOWSKI

Jennifer is an artist who creates incredible patterns and beautiful paintings. Her work has a Mid-Century Modern look and she creates it with both digital and traditional methods.

Tulip II *by Jennifer Skoropowski*

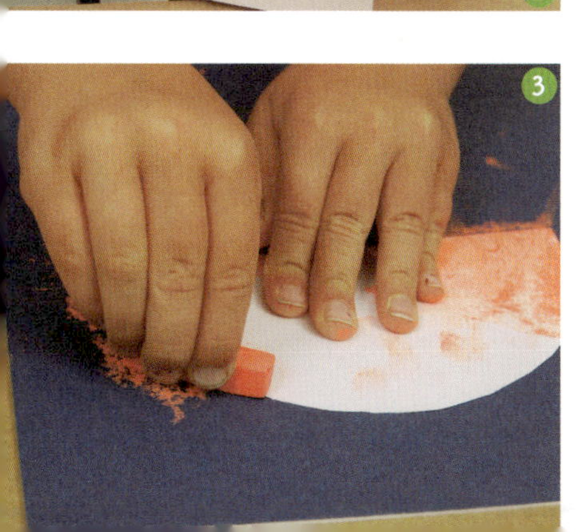

LET'S MAKE ART!

1. Place the round container half on and half off the side of the cover stock. Trace around the half circle on the cover stock with a pencil.
2. Cut out the half circle. This is now your template.
3. Place the template on the background paper. Hold the chalk pastel on its side. Push the pastel from the center of the template out past the edge all around the half circle.
4. Move the half circle to another position and continue making umbrella tops.
5. Cut out handle shapes from colored papers and glue on.
6. Have an adult spray the final piece with fixative outside.

EXPLORE MORE

Make rectangles for templates to create buildings or triangles to create a pyramid!

Spring Relief Painting

MATERIALS

- Masonite board
- Joint compound
- Palette knife
- Pussy willow branches or twigs
- Wooden skewer
- Watercolor pans
- Watercolor brush
- Newspaper
- Water container

INSPIRED BY BRIDGETTE GUERZON MILLS

Bridgette Guerzon Mills is an award winning mixed media artist who has exhibited her work nationally and internationally. Her work incorporates a variety of media including photography, encaustic and salvaged materials. Her paintings, journals, and book art have been published in magazines and books and her work has been collected in the United States and abroad. She currently resides in Towson, MD with her family.

Lifeline *by Bridgette Guerzon Mills*

GET READY!

Select twigs or as we did, pussy willow boughs to press into the painting. Think about how they will look in your painting. Keep joint compound off your hands and wash hands thoroughly after use.

LET'S MAKE ART!

1. Break your twigs or pussy willows to fit or slightly longer than the Masonite board.

2. Arrange them as you like! You are the artist!

3. Apply the join compound to the board with a palette knife and spread to the edges.

4. Draw a horizon line or other marks with the skewer to show where your pussy willows are growing.

5. Push your pussy willows into the joint compound and add any additional lines. Let dry overnight.

6. Paint the background with watercolor to finish.

EXPLORE MORE

Joint compound can hold small pebbles, shells, seeds and acorns. Your painting can develop around the objects you find.

Garden Tile

MATERIALS

- Low fire stoneware clay or oven-bake clay
- Scoring tool
- Circle cookie cutter
- Paper
- Scissors
- Clay pin tool
- Underglaze or acrylic paint
- Ruler
- Wire
- Strong glue
- Clear glaze

EXPLORE MORE

There is no end to the variety of nature inspired tiles you can make. Try changing the shape of the tile. Create your favorite insects or animals likenesses and add them to the tile.

INSPIRED BY THE AUTHOR, SUSAN SCHWAKE

I have made tiles for our own garden and for gifts for so long that I always have one or two hanging around the studio. The enthusiasm for tile making runs high with our students and is a good first lesson in working with clay.

Garden Fence *by Susan Schwake*

GET READY!

In the spring, before the plants begin to flower, it is nice to have a cheery reminder of what is to come. These tiles can be hung on a garden wall or fence or you can enjoy them year-round indoors.

LET'S MAKE ART!

1. Roll out a slab of clay as explained in the recipes section.
2. Cut out a tile-shaped pattern from paper, the size you want the tile to be.
3. Lay the paper on the clay slab and cut around it.
4. Using the circle cutter on the remaining clay, cut out the flower petals and centers. Cut the circles in half with the pin tool to make petals.
5. Decide where your flowers will go on the tile.
6. Attach the flowers to the tile using the scoring tool to roughen up both surfaces first, so they stick to each other. Press each piece down firmly too!
7. Use an underglaze to add color and detail to your tile and fire at the appropriate temperature.
8. Attach a wire to the back with strong glue (we use E6000 with the help of an adult) to hang.

May Baskets

MATERIALS

- Materials
- Card stock
- Oil pastels
- Watercolor pans
- Paper doily
- Glue stick
- Stapler
- Assorted flowers and candy

INSPIRED BY TRADITION

When I was a little girl we made May baskets on May 1st to give to our friends. We would hook them over the doorknob on their front door and ring the bell – then run! My children made them as well, as it was our way of sweetly heralding in the spring with our friends.

Traditional May basket on a doorknob

GET READY!

Each May basket can be personalized with a special drawing. Consider a few options before starting. Make a list of who you are making baskets for and gather the goodies for inside each one.

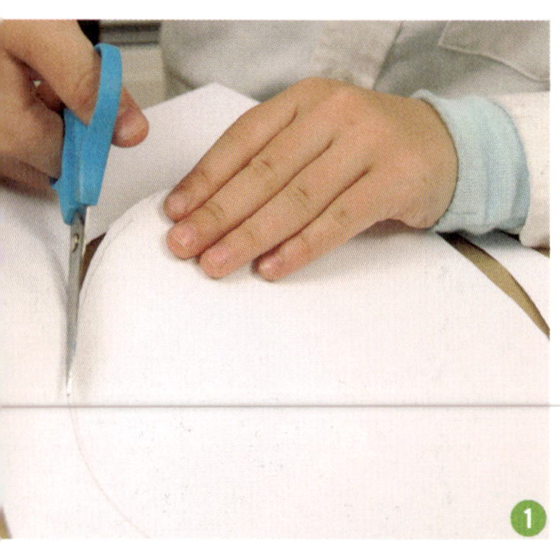

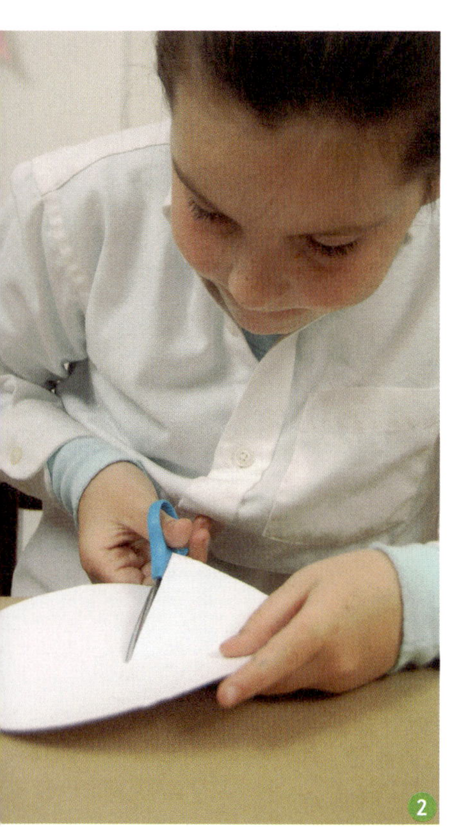

LET'S MAKE ART!

1. Cut a circle out of the card stock.
2. Cut a slit from one side to the center.
3. Make a cone and mark the edge where the paper ends.
4. Cut a strip for the handle across the width of the card stock

EXPLORE MORE

These May baskets can be filled with any small treasures you can think of! Try a tiny live plant inside a plastic bag or some packages of flower seeds.

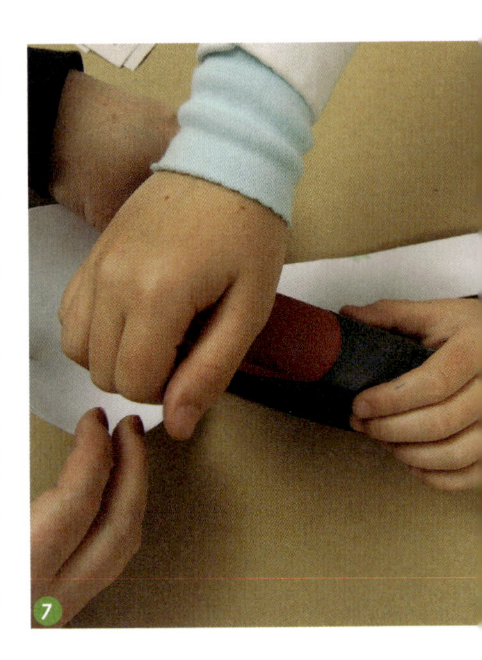

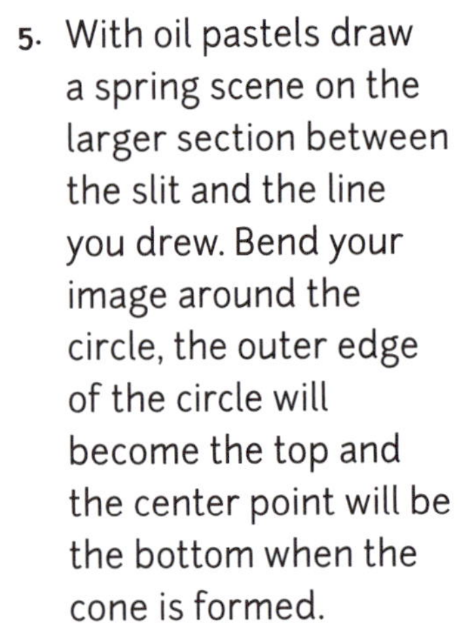

5. With oil pastels draw a spring scene on the larger section between the slit and the line you drew. Bend your image around the circle, the outer edge of the circle will become the top and the center point will be the bottom when the cone is formed.

6. Go over the oil pastels with watercolor and a wet brush. Let dry.

7. Make the cone and secure with a staple.

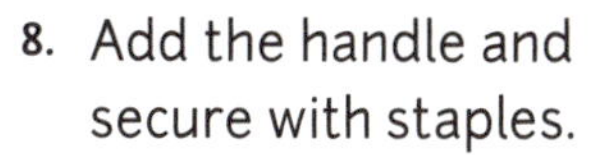

8. Add the handle and secure with staples.

9. Cut the doily in half and secure each half inside using a glue stick.

10. Fill the cone with tiny fresh flowers and candy and give to a friend.

Relief Printed Cards

MATERIALS

- Safety-cut lino
- Lino cutting tools
- Pencil
- Paper
- Water-based block printmaking ink
- Newspaper
- Cookie sheet
- Bench hook

GET READY!

Printmaking is a way of creating original multiples of your art. It is a great method for making greeting cards to send to your friends in Spring or any time of the year. Always make sure that your hands are behind your cutting tools and use a bench hook when carving your block. Fold the card stock in half to have it ready to print.

INSPIRED BY JENNIFER HEWETT

Jen Hewett is a self-taught, San Francisco-based printmaker and surface designer. Working out of her tiny studio, Jen screenprints and block prints her bright, colorful work on fabric, and then sews it into bags and pillows. Stores throughout the US carry her bags, and her products have made their way to destinations all over the world.

Wisteria *by Jen Hewett*

LET'S MAKE ART!

1. Begin by drawing your design out on a piece of paper within the size of your lino block.

2. Redraw your design onto the lino with a pencil.

3. With pencil, fill in the areas that you will cut away. What is left will be raised up and becomes your design.

4. Using the bench hook and keep your hands behind the cutting tool, carve away the areas that are not part of your design leaving the raised design that you will print.

EXPLORE MORE

You can print your carved block on a tee shirt or tote bag. Use textile ink to print with and follow the instructions on the label for setting the ink.

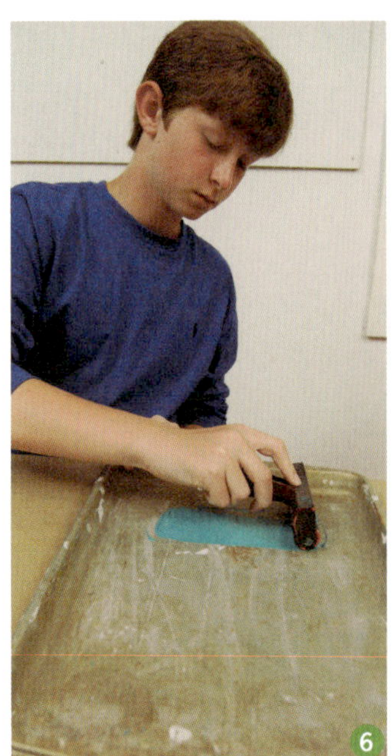

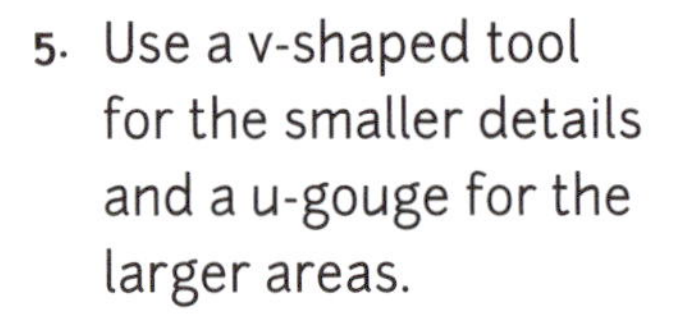

5. Use a v-shaped tool for the smaller details and a u-gouge for the larger areas.

6. Roll out some ink onto the cookie sheet until smooth.

7. Roll the ink over the carved block until covered.

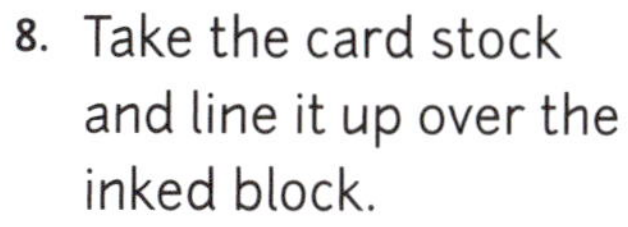

8. Take the card stock and line it up over the inked block.

9. Press firmly with your fingertips all over the inside of the folded card stock. Make sure to contact all parts of the block.

10. Holding the card stock in place, lift one corner to check if the print is as you want it to be.

11. Pull your print off the block

12. Repeat the printing process to make more cards.

Pysanky Eggs

MATERIALS

- Wooden eggs (most craft stores have them)
- Oil pastels
- Sketch paper
- Pencil
- Watercolor pans
- Water container
- Soft brush

INSPIRED BY ANDREA KULISH

Andrea is a first-generation Ukrainian-American who has been making pysanky since she was six years old. She is an artist, craftsperson, photographer and graphic design professional. After college, she was based in Boston for 21 years, and has recently relocated to North Carolina.

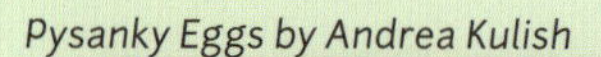

Pysanky Eggs by Andrea Kulish

GET READY!

Check out a book from your local library on the traditional art of Pysanky egg decorating. There are many different traditional and contemporary designs to explore! Pysanky egg decorating works much in the same way as our lesson. Using a special kistka tool, hot wax is dispensed onto the egg and the layers of dye and wax are built up and then removed, to create beautiful designs.

LET'S MAKE ART!

1. First draw out a few of your ideas for designs with pencil on paper.
2. Choose your favorite designs to draw onto the wooden eggs.
3. Use oil pastels and press firmly when drawing on the eggs to create a clear line.
4. Using a wet brush loaded with plenty of watercolor, paint over the whole egg. The oil pastel will resist the watercolor, so your design will show through.

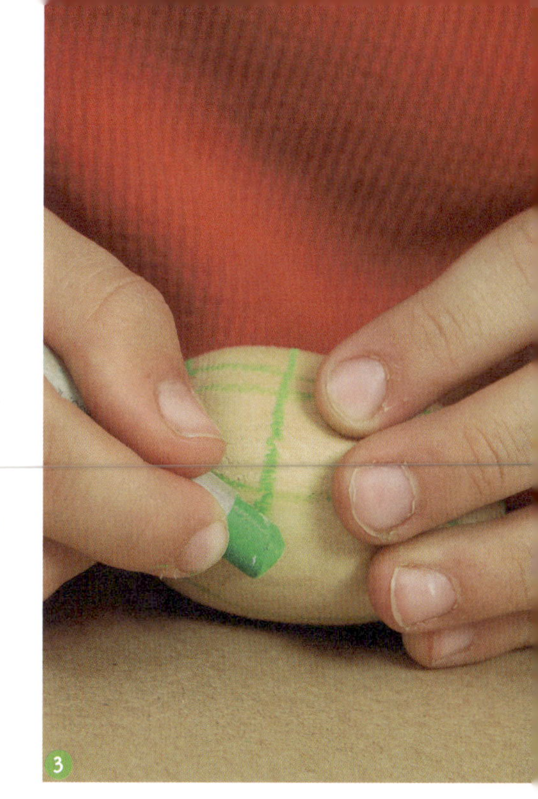

EXPLORE MORE

Try making a dozen eggs using all traditional patterns that you have researched.

Bugs!

MATERIALS

- Pleated coffee filter
- Watercolor pans
- Watercolor brush
- Flat clothespin
- Chenille stems
- Beads
- Embroidery floss
- Hot glue (to be used by adult)
- Newspaper
- Water container

GET READY!

Making sculptures of insects that we see in our gardens can be fun. With this project you can make them as realistic or fanciful as you wish!

INSPIRED BY CILLA STILES

I enjoy creating art that is tactile and dimensional. I love browsing through old natural history museums full of moth eaten specimens. For years, I have been creating fantastical specimens of insects, fish and birds. I've filled antique wooden cabinets with them: my version of a cabinet of curiosities, complete with Latin names. I also have framed groupings on my walls.

Gilda *by Cilla Stiles*

EXPLORE MORE

You can try cutting the ends of the wings into different shapes to make different-looking wings! Try two sets of wings – one cut smaller – to mimic a dragonfly.

LET'S MAKE ART!

1. Set up your painting station as described in the recipe section. Smooth the coffee filter flat.

2. Begin painting the coffee filter with the pattern you choose.
3. Fill the filter with as much color as you like! Let dry.
4. Wind the chenille stem around the clothespin to cover the length of it. Glue the end of the chenille stem to the clothespin.

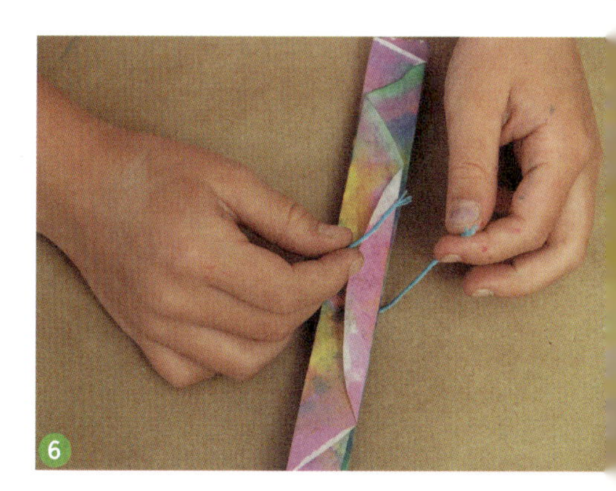

5. Fold the filter back and forth as you would a paper fan or accordion fashion.
6. Tie the middle of the folded filter with a piece of embroidery floss to cinch it. Knot it tightly!
7. Glue on the eyes to the head of the clothespin and glue the wings to the back of the clothes pin with the hot glue.
8. Glue the bug to a piece of mat board or wood to finish.

Wrapped Vase

MATERIALS

- Low fire clay
- Lace or doilies
- Rolling pin
- Pin tool
- Scoring tool
- Circle cutter
- Ruler
- Soft Sponge
- Soft brush
- Water container
- Underglaze
- Clear glaze

GET READY!

Spring always means flowers, so why not celebrate them by making a special vase for them? You can use any lace or a crocheted doily that can be found at a thrift store or perhaps your grandmother's attic!

INSPIRED BY MEGAN BOGONOVICH

Megan Bogonovich is a New Hampshire artist whose big ceramic sculptures have drawn international attention. Her work often has repeated patterns and textural details beyond what you can imagine. She makes functional ware that demands different tools, so she makes them as she goes along. Megan lives and works in Concord, NH.

Vase by Megan Bogonovich

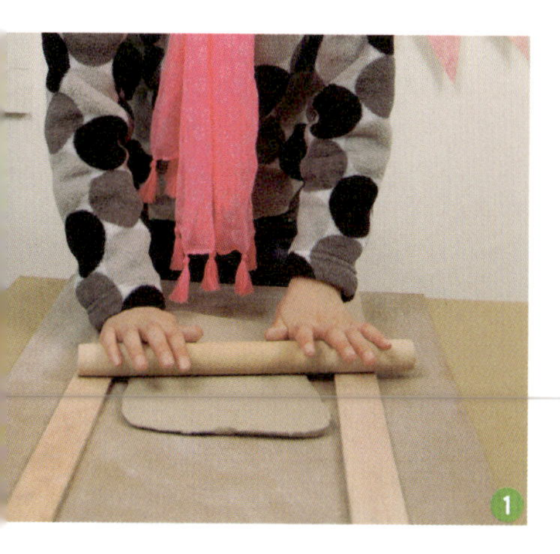

LET'S MAKE ART!

1. Roll out a slab of clay (as shown in the recipes section) Flip it but do not turn it-we want a long piece for wrapping.

2. Using the circle cutter, cut one circle from one end of the slab. Cut close to the edge to conserve clay.

3. Using a ruler lengthwise, cut a long strip of clay about 2 inches (5 cm) wide. This will be the first layer of the vase.

4. Cut another strip of clay slightly larger than the first.

5. Put the doily or lace on top of one of the strips and roll over it firmly to make the texture of the doily imprint into the clay. Repeat with the second strip of clay.

6. Using the scoring tool, rough up the sides of the clay circle all the way around.

EXPLORE MORE

You can make much taller vases by building more clay strips up around the vase. Try different textures from nature such as bark, leaves and flowers.

Wrapped Vase

7

8

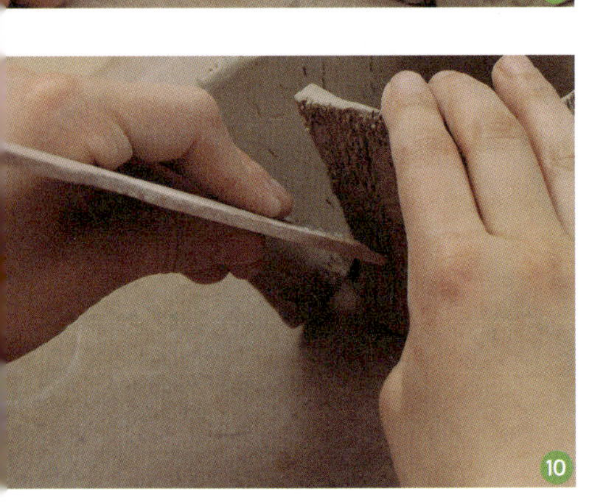

10

7. Using the scoring tool, rough up the inside bottom edge of the first strip of clay.
8. Wrap the strip of clay around the circle, pressing firmly where the two pieces meet. Trim it if the strip is too long.
9. Score the strip on BOTH sides of the ends where they meet.
10. Press the seam firmly to join the two pieces together.
11. Score the second strip of clay along its length and score the outside top of the first layer. Attach them together and press firmly as you go.
12. Finish the ends as before.

11

12

13. Smooth the inside where the two layers meet, supporting it with your other hand on the outside of the vase.

14. Turn it upside down and gently smooth the bottom of the pot to the side wall. Smooth from the center to the edge to seal. Let dry

15. Apply the underglaze to the pot. Use the colors of your choice. Fire at the appropriate temperature.

16. Add a second color of underglaze over the sections you desire. We used green over the black. Let dry.

17. Using a damp sponge, wipe the glaze off gently to expose the color below. The new color will stay in the grooved areas of the texture!

18. Add the final clear glaze and fire to the appropriate temperature.

SUMMER

SUMMER

Summer is full of inspiration – everywhere you look. The rivers and lakes are sparkling and full of life and the ocean waves crashing on the sand bringing us treasures worn smooth. It is a time when nature puts on her most colorful attire and blossoms with perfume, buzzes with song and flies on stained glass wings. To take a walk in a field in the summer is to fill all the senses with inspiration.

Hike up a mountain and gain new perspective. Sit quietly in a garden and observe the tiniest of creatures. Float down a river or paddle into a lake to explore the shoreline from the other side. Even at night there is something spectacular to see - look up to see the tiny fireflies in the trees mimicking the stars above them. Take notes, make sketches and keep an eye out for art all around you!

Feather Paintings

MATERIALS

- Small canvas board
- Brayer
- Acrylic paint
- Newspaper
- Feather
- Toothbrush
- Water container

EXPLORE MORE

Try painting with other tools from nature such as a soft pine branch used as a brush or dip acorn tops and seed pods as texture printing tools!

INSPIRED BY THE AUTHOR, SUSAN SCHWAKE

I love using alternative painting tools to create paintings with. In this painting I have used bark and feathers to give the landscape texture.

At the Marsh *by Susan Schwake*

GET READY!

Paint with a feather? Spatter with a toothbrush? These alternative painting tools can free your imagination!

LET'S MAKE ART!

1. Place the canvas board on top of some newspaper to protect the surfaces. Put four or six small dabs of acrylic paint on your canvas.

2. Using the brayer, roll out the paint to mix it and cover the entire canvas with color

3. Choose a different color of paint and thin it with a little water so the paint is about the consistency of cream. Dip the end of the feather into the paint.

4. Make strokes with the end of the feather and dip again to continue painting.

5. Choose another color of paint and thin as above. Dip the toothbrush bristles into the paint.

6. Point the brush down towards the canvas and gently run your thumb over the bristles to spatter paint onto the painting.

7. Continue until you are pleased with the composition.

Relief Sand Castings

MATERIALS

- Materials
- Small box (we used a greeting card box)
- Sand
- Shells
- Plaster
- Plastic bowl for mixing plaster
- Paint stirrer
- Bristle brush

INSPIRED BY ADAM PEARSON

Adam is a Barrington, New Hampshire, sculptor and craftsman. He often uses found metals for his sculptures and creates bronze castings.

Figures *by Adam Pearson*

GET READY!

A summer's day at the shore often ends with a special pile of shells or rocks that have been found. Drift wood and sea glass are sweet tokens from a trip to the beach, too. Casting a few of these items in plaster can remind you of summer all year round. This lesson combines the excitement of casting and found objects as a sculptural material. Have an adult on hand to help with the plaster.

LET'S MAKE ART!

1. Fill your box ¾ of the way full with sand.
2. Arrange your shells and make prints with them in the sand.
3. Mix plaster according to the directions on the package.
4. Pour plaster into the box slowly. Extra plaster should be left to harden and disposed of properly. Do not put plaster down the drain.
5. You may use a plastic cup to pour the first layer of plaster slowly to avoid floating shells. With the stirrer, push down any shells that float to the top.
6. Let the plaster set fully. Rip the box off the plaster cast.
7. Brush away the extra sand with the bristle brush to expose your relief sculpture.

EXPLORE MORE

Any small bit of nature that you find can be cast this way. Try adding a variety of small driftwood pieces or pebbles you have collected.

Record Mandala

MATERIALS

- Gesso
- Phonograph record
- Foam brush
- Acrylic paint
- Paint brushes: large and small
- Paint markers
- Newspapers

EXPLORE MORE

Try making a rainbow mandala. Try making a pattern from different insects or your favorite leaves.

INSPIRED BY CADA DRISCOLL

Cada guides students in creativity and creates artwork herself by the seacoast in New England. Her work is inspired by an abiding love of nature, community, and life!

Glimmer Mandala *by Cada Driscoll*

GET READY!

The word mandala comes from Sanskrit meaning "circle". Circles are found everywhere in nature and are a wonderful change for a painting surface from the standard rectangle. For our mandala we repurposed a discarded phonograph record. You can find them at yard sales and at your local thrift shops. Using a repetitive pattern and featuring our favorite flowers, this mandala celebrates Summer's bounty.

LET'S MAKE ART!

1. Prime the record with gesso using the foam brush. Let dry.

2. Paint the background first using one or more colors.

3. Start at the center or the outer edge of the record to paint your designs. Let dry between patterns to keep from smudging.

4. Use the paint pens for the smallest details and the brushes for larger strokes.

5. Finish the smallest details. Let dry and hang on the wall!

Sun Prints

GET READY!

You can recreate a scene from nature or simply print interesting patterns by arranging gathered flora on this sun-sensitive paper. The objects you choose will make silhouettes where they are placed.

- Cyanotype paper
- Flowers, leaves and grasses
- Shallow pan of water
- Cardboard

INSPIRED BY JUDITH HELLER CASSELL

Judith Heller Cassell is an artist from New Hampshire who specializes in printmaking. Nature is abundant in her work. We often exhibit her prints in our gallery.

Willow 4 *by Judith Heller Cassell*

LET'S MAKE ART!

1. Gather fallen flower petals, weeds, grass, leaves and other interesting plants from your yard.
2. Open packet of the sun-sensitive paper while you are indoors and place paper blue side up on the cardboard for support. The indoor lighting will not expose the paper.
3. Arrange the nature items on paper and take outside to expose to the sun until the paper turns very pale blue (about two to five minutes).
4. Bring inside and place the paper in the water. Gently move the paper back and forth until the paper darkens.
5. Slip the paper back on the cardboard to dry.

EXPLORE MORE

The print can be mounted on card stock for a special greeting card or put in a frame as a print!

Breezy Wind Chimes

MATERIALS

- Low fire clay
- Under glaze
- Circle and square cookie cutters
- Rolling pin
- Guides
- Masonite / fiberboard
- Foam tray
- String
- Small tree branch
- Soft paintbrush
- Water container

EXPLORE MORE

Try making a lot of shapes to create a very long wind chime that you could hang from a tree. Make sure to bring the chimes indoors if it gets below freezing in your area. They can hang quietly all winter on a wall!

GET READY!

Wind chimes are found all over the world. We love the sounds they make in a summer breeze. These wind chimes have a lovely modern form as well as a soft tinkling sound.

INSPIRED BY JAPANESE WIND CHIMES

These Japanese wind chimes have animal shapes cast into the metal. You could try making clay wind chimes in animal shapes, too!

Wind chimes in Nagano, Japan

LET'S MAKE ART!

1. Roll out a slab as shown in the recipes section.

2. Using the cutters, cut out at least a dozen or more assorted shapes from the clay slab.

3. Make sure to put a hole in the solid shapes for hanging, both at the top and the bottom.

4. Place them in the foam tray and brush on the underglaze on both sides. Bisque fire to appropriate temperatures.

5. Arrange the clay shapes into three lines as you would like them to hang from the branch. Try a few different patterns to see what you like best.

6. String them together and tie each to the branch. Tie a string to both ends of the branch to hang up your wind chime.

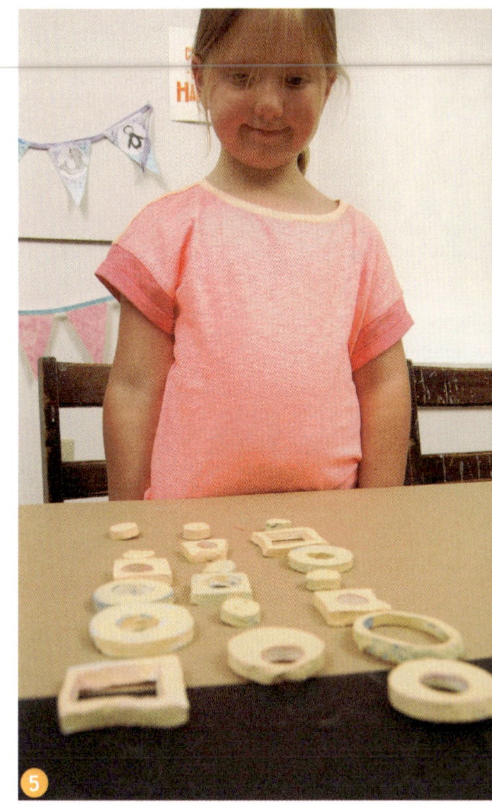

MATERIALS

- Acrylic paint
- Paint palette or plastic egg carton
- Assorted brushes
- Water containers
- Newspaper
- Stretched canvas

INSPIRED BY ASHLEY GOLDBERG

Ashley G is a prolific and popular artist creating wonderful patterns, sweet and mysterious paintings and is one of the top sellers on Etsy. This beautiful painting from her sketches is but one reason I fell in love with her work. She is also one of the nicest artists I know!

Fireworks *by Ashley Goldberg*

GET READY!

Sometimes color alone can inspire us to paint. For this lesson, we let the colors and shapes of summer guide us freely. Some of the shapes could come from life or from your imagination.

LET'S MAKE ART!

1. Choose your first color and create some shapes using your whole arm – be free with the strokes. The shapes may or may not look like anything from life. Our artist chose a flower-like shape.

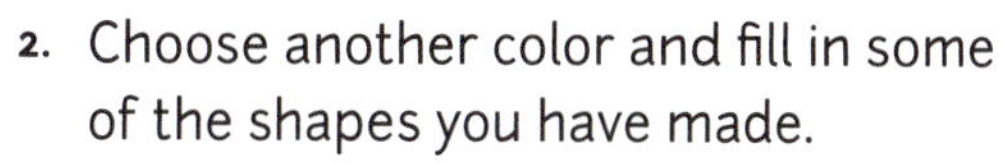

2. Choose another color and fill in some of the shapes you have made.
3. Choose another color and continue filling in the shapes or making new shapes.
4. Let dry. Take a step back from the painting and decide what details you want to add. Tiny shapes or long lines similar to other marks you have made? It's up to you as the artist!
5. Let your painting dry between layers. Add as much or as little detail as you like. Be free and let Summer just flow out of your brush!

EXPLORE MORE

This lesson can be repeated using small canvases or large pieces of paper and different sizes of brushes. Go extra big and use a house painting brush on a wall-sized paper!

Bubble Fish Mobile

MATERIALS

- Materials
- Bubble Wrap
- Watercolor pans
- Soft brush
- Card stock
- Embroidery hoop
- Embroidery floss
- Clear glue
- Needle
- White adhesive dots
- Markers
- Scissors
- Pencil
- Ruler

INSPIRED BY JENNIFER SKOROPOWSKI

Jennifer is an artist who creates incredible patterns and beautiful paintings. Her work has a Mid-Century Modern look and she creates it with both digital and traditional methods.

Tiki Tok Fish *by Jennifer Skoropowski*

GET READY!

Mobiles are sculptures that move. The simple shape of a fish gives this mobile a modern look. Printing with bubble wrap adds to the repeating circles patterns found in this sculpture.

LET'S MAKE ART!

1. Paint a strip of bubble wrap with the watercolor paints.
2. Flip the painted side of the bubble wrap onto the cover stock to print it.
3. Continue until the paper is printed on both sides.
4. Section the paper off with a ruler along the length of the printed paper to create one-inch strips.
5. Cut strips across the short end of the paper. Fold each strip in half.

EXPLORE MORE

Try making a miniature version of this by starting with smaller paper and tiny dots.

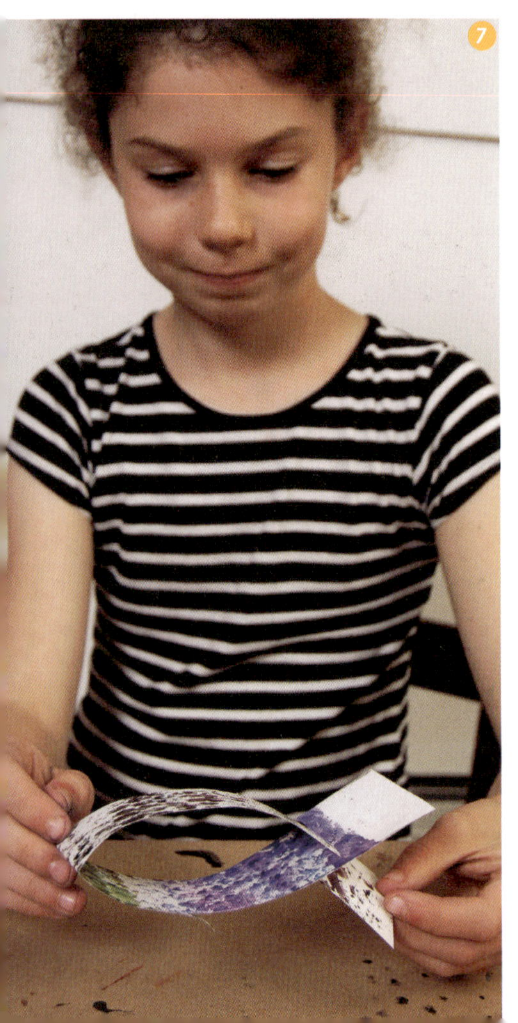

6. Cut a slit on the top of one end and the bottom of the other end of each strip. Interlock the ends to create the fish form.

7. Adjust the fish form by pushing on both ends.

8. Thread the needle with the embroidery floss and push the needle from the bottom of the fish through the top. Add a drop of glue to the top of the fish, to hold in place. Add as many fish on each thread as you wish in the same manner.

9. Tie the end of the embroidery floss from each string of fish to the hoop.

10. Cut three lengths of embroidery floss to create a hanger for the mobile. Position them in a triangle formation to hang evenly.

11. Color a sheet of white adhesive dots with a marker.

12. Hang your mobile up and add the dots to the strings of fish by sticking them back-to-back along the embroidery floss.

Drawing Nature

MATERIALS

- Leaves, bark, acorns, seed pods, pebbles, flowers, feathers or other nature items
- Set of colored pencils
- Pencil
- Eraser
- Drawing paper

EXPLORE MORE

Challenge yourself by creating a still life with many objects. Give yourself plenty of time to draw so you are not rushed.

GET READY!

Choose your favorite nature items from the woods, your yard, the shore or a garden. Lay them out naturally or next to each other in rows. This is called creating the composition and it's your choice as the artist!

INSPIRED BY HEATHER SMITH JONES

Heather Smith Jones, MFA, is an artist working in painting, drawing, photography, and printmaking. She is an instructor at an arts-based preschool and the author of *Water Paper Paint, Exploring Creativity with Watercolor and Mixed Media*. Smith Jones lives in Lawrence, KS with her husband and their four felines.

I remember *Heather Smith Jones*

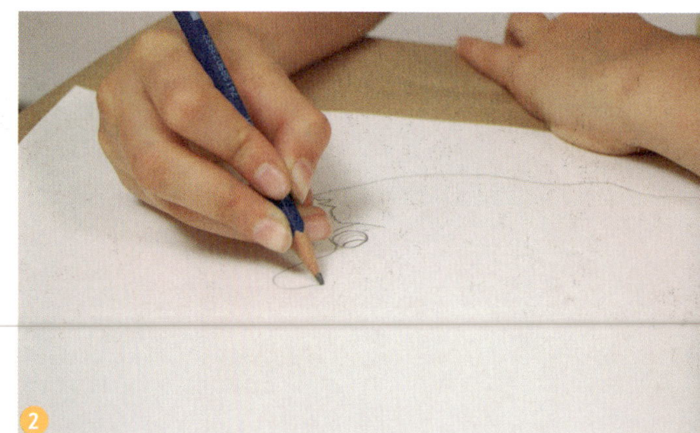

LET'S MAKE ART!

1. Begin your drawing by taking a few moments to look closely at the still life objects. What shapes are they?

2. Draw the larger shaped objects first with the pencil.

3. Draw lightly with the pencil and keep checking your lines as you go. Drawing lightly makes it easy to erase if you need to!

4. Remember to pick up the pencil where your objects overlap.

5. Look for details which show texture or special features of the object you are drawing.

6. When you are satisfied with the pencil drawing, begin to add color with the colored pencils.

7. Don't press too hard! Try building up the color slowly by coloring light layers.

8. You can place your still life objects into an imaginary setting if you wish.

Painting Outside

GET READY!

Choose a location outside that interests you to paint "en plein air" – this is the French expression for painting outside in the open air. This lesson gives you a chance to paint what you see directly and spontaneously. Make sure you have a place for your easel and paint supplies so you are comfortable while painting.

MATERIALS

- Canvas
- Easel
- Pencil
- Acrylic paint
- Chair or table
- Newspaper
- Assorted brushes
- Water container
- Palette paper

EXPLORE MORE

Your own backyard or a park can be a wonderful place to paint. If you live near a lake or the ocean you could try painting there too!

INSPIRED BY CHRISTOPHER VOLPE

Christopher Volpe paints and teaches oil painting year-round both en plein air and in the studio. With a graduate degree in poetry, he taught college English and art history for several years before falling in love with American landscape painting and becoming a professional artist.

A River Finds A Way (Vermont) by Chris Volpe

LET'S MAKE ART!

1. Start by taking a good look at what you are going to paint. Where does the sky meet the land? Where do the main objects in the painting go? What parts are in the shade?

2. Begin drawing the landscape lightly with pencil.

3. Once you are satisfied with your drawing begin painting the background. Have up your palette and water station on a chair or small table next to you.

4. Continue painting from the background to the foreground without adding tiny details.

5. Once you have covered all the white canvas, begin painting the second layer. Add darker and lighter areas depending on where the light falls on your subject matter. Pay attention to details. Keep looking at your reference in front of you.

6. Finish your painting by adding any further details you observe.

Button Fish

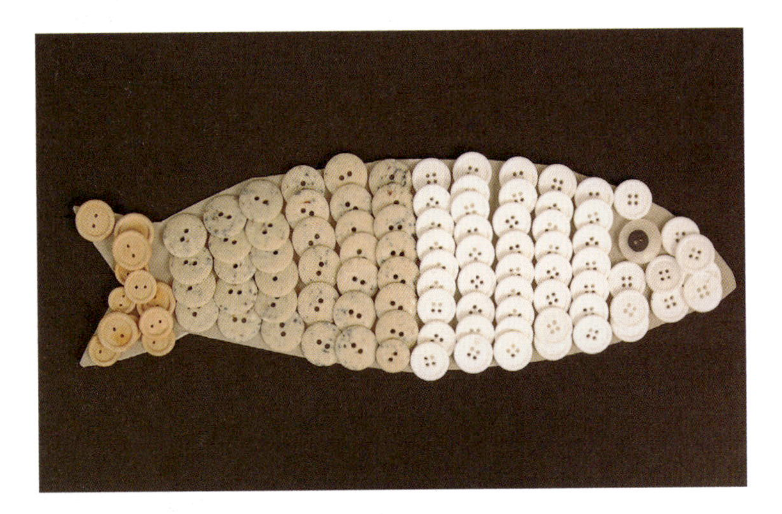

MATERIALS

- Lightweight cardboard
- Scissors
- Assorted buttons
- Clear tacky glue
- Mat board

EXPLORE MORE

You could make a fish in the same fashion using collected bottle caps!

GET READY!

Fish are a wide variety of shapes and sizes. Study them in an aquarium or in books and decide what shape your art will take! Collect as many buttons as you can to create your fish.

INSPIRED BY THE BUTTON KING

Dalton Stevens better known as *The Button King* is known for his button art. He has sewn and glued buttons onto his guitar, suits and even cars! Find out more about this self-taught artist at his website: www.scbuttonking.com

LET'S MAKE ART!

1. Choose the buttons that you want for your fish.

2. Draw a fish shape on a piece of thin cardboard and cut it out. This will be your support for the fish.

3. Layout the buttons on the fish. Make a pattern with the buttons to show stripes or sections as desired.

4. Use smaller sized buttons for smaller areas of the fish, such as the tail.

5. After your layout is ready, begin to glue the buttons on one row at a time.

6. For the eye, try stacking two buttons of different sizes. Glue securely.

7. Stack buttons, if desired, on the fin or tail areas.

8. Finish by mounting the fish to a piece of wood or mat board.

AUTUMN

AUTUMN

Trees ablaze with color here in New England bring people from all over the world to view nature's spectacle of Autumn. Our finest hours are crisp outdoor air filled with birds flying south and squirrels stashing nuts away for winter. The last hot days are revered with trips to the lake and campfires with sparks flying high. There are golden hayfields and patches of farms filled with pumpkins and squash vines. Apple trees are full of fruits and walking through an orchard in Autumn is a delight for the senses.

The crunch of the leaves in late Autumn with the scent of a woodstove burning are familiar to those of us who walk the woods here in New England. The skies are a little bluer with the orange and reds of the trees intersecting them, the hills a little brighter with the last long rays of a sunny day shining on them. Spend some time deep into Autumn looking for that special part of nature that sparks a drawing or creates an idea to sculpt – it's there waiting for you.

Clay Totem Poles

GET READY!

Totem poles are found in the Pacific Northwest region of North America. Check your local library for books about the history of totem poles and the animals carved into them!

MATERIALS

- Oven bake clay
- Acrylic paint
- Paint markers
- Skewer
- Strong glue
- Section of a tree branch
- Brushes
- Newspaper
- Water container

EXPLORE MORE

Totem poles come in many sizes. Try making a larger one – use a skewer as a support through the middle of each animal. Try adding wings.

INSPIRED BY THE FIRST NATION PEOPLE

The First Nation people of the Pacific Northwest created some of the most beautiful and sacred totem poles. Check your local library to learn more about them.

Two totem poles in the Nimkish village Yilis, on Cormorant Island.

LET'S MAKE ART!

1. Draw your ideas out first. Find references for the animals you choose. Start with three favorite animals.

2. Using the oven bake clay begin with three equal pieces. Make sure the pieces will fit well on the wooden base

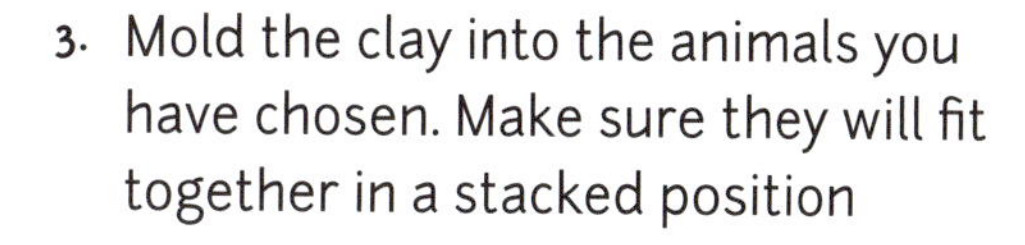

3. Mold the clay into the animals you have chosen. Make sure they will fit together in a stacked position

4. Use a wooden skewer for making details. Bake according to package directions

5. Paint with acrylic paint as desired. Use paint markers for details.

6. With the help of an adult glue the pieces together (we used E6000) to create the totem pole. Glue to base and let dry.

Place Cards

MATERIALS

- Materials
- Card board or mat board
- Gold paint
- Thin soft brush
- Black fine point marker
- Copy paper
- Scissors
- Pencil
- Acorns or leaves for reference
- Salt dough
- Clear finish spray (to be used outside)

INSPIRED BY LISA CONGDON

Lisa Congdon is a mixed media artist and illustrator from Oakland, California. She illustrates for such clients as Martha Stewart Living and The Museum of Modern Art, among others. She is the author of *Whatever You Are, Be a Good One, and Art Inc.* Much of her work is inspired by both nature and folk pattern.

Jonathan Swift *by Lisa Congdon*

GET READY!

The art of hand drawn letters is a delightful change from using the computer all the time. Why not celebrate a special harvest meal with a hand drawn place card for each guest? Research different typefaces or make up your own.

LET'S MAKE ART!

1. Choose at typeface or make one up and practice it on your paper with pencil.
2. Cut your cardboard or mat board to the size you would like. We used scrap mat board from the local frame shop.
3. Draw the names lightly in pencil as a guide. Outline them with black marker.
4. Add gold paint with a thin brush to accent the letters.
5. Illustrate the name with acorns or leaves to embellish.
6. Create a holder for the card with a ball of salt dough. Place the card in the middle to create a slit for it to stand on.
7. With the help of an adult bake dough at 350° F until hard and coat with clear finish outside.

EXPLORE MORE

Once you start lettering it's hard to stop! Try lettering a short poem or saying that you like and illustrate it as desired. Check your library for books about Calligraphy – the art of writing.

Woodland Mask

MATERIALS

- Lightweight cardboard
- Assorted colored papers
- Cardboard tubes
- Tacky Glue
- Scissors
- Acrylic paint
- Gesso
- Water container
- Masking tape
- Newspaper
- Flour
- Plastic bowl

GET READY

Mask making is a common thread found in every culture all around the world. The masks we will make can be decorative or they can be worn. Choose an animal or make up a character that you might find in the fall.

INSPIRED BY JEANNÉ MCCARTIN

Jeanné is a New Hampshire based artist who often creates masks. Jeanné says: Masks have long been used to manifest the natural. They are also used for decoration, sacred ritual, and transformation. They hide and reveal, may be worn as protection and are a language of both honesty and deceit. Masks are also an endless source of exploration for an artist; reason enough to create them.

Harvest King *by Jeanné McCartin*

LET'S MAKE ART!

1. Draw out a few ideas before you begin. Choose one and gather materials.
2. Draw a face shape on the cardboard. Cut it out. This will be the base of the mask.
3. At each end of the face shape cut a v-shaped notch.
4. On each side of the face shape, fold the edges in towards the center. Cut out eye shapes.

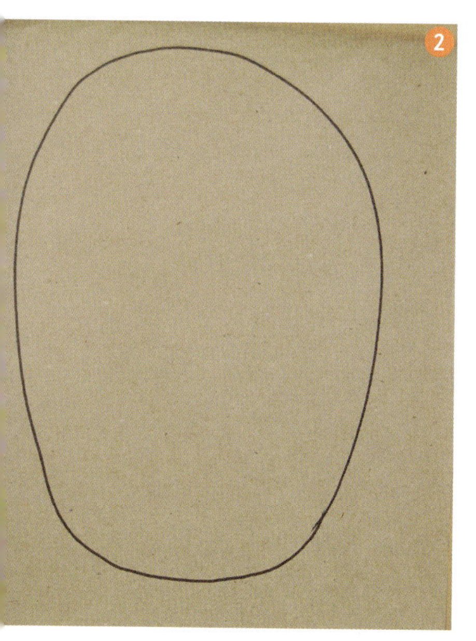

EXPLORE MORE

These masks can be even larger. Make the base from a heavier weight of cardboard and create some really big art!

5. On each end of the face shape, fold the v-shaped notches to create a forehead and chin. Secure with masking tape on both sides.

6. Build up the face with paper tubes. Make the features pop! Make short cuts around the tube and fold them out to make a tab or flange. This makes it easy to tape onto the mask.

7. Mix up the papier-mâché goo, from the recipe section. Tear strips of newspaper. Support the mask with additional tubes or balls of newspaper, on a newspaper-covered surface.

8. Dip the strips of newspaper into the goo and remove excess. Begin applying the strips to the mask base.

9. Let dry completely. Paint the entire mask with gesso to cover the newsprint and seal it.

10. Paint the mask with acrylic paint as desired.

11. Use the colored paper to create additional embellishments.

12. Glue on embellishments with the Tacky Glue and let dry.

- Fresh leaves
- Card stock
- Watercolor pans
- Soft paint brush
- Water container
- Newspaper

INSPIRED BY HEATHER SMITH JONES

Heather Smith Jones, MFA, is an artist working in painting, drawing, photography, and printmaking. She is an instructor at an arts-based preschool and the author of Water Paper Paint, Exploring Creativity with Watercolor and Mixed Media. Smith Jones lives in Lawrence, KS with her husband and their four felines.

All Things New *by Heather Smith Jones*

GET READY!

Choose a variety of leaves for this project. Small clusters of leaves work as well as one large leaf.

LET'S MAKE ART!

1. Lay your leaves out in a pattern that appeals to you.

2. Using a wet brush and plenty of watercolor, brush your first leaf from the center over the edge all the way around the edges.

3. Hold the leaf firmly to the paper.

4. Continue with the rest of the leaves.

5. Let dry between layers. Try overlapping a leaf or making a pile.

Try simple shaped flower petals in the same fashion. Turn your creations into special greeting cards.

Stitched Family Portraits

MATERIALS

- Muslin cotton
- Embroidery hoop
- Embroidery floss in assorted colors
- Embroidery needles
- Photograph to fit inside hoop
- Masking tape
- Scissors
- Pencil

EXPLORE MORE

Use one color for the whole piece for a monochromatic look. Make a pet portrait of your family pet!

INSPIRED BY LISA SOLOMON

"I think that my work is fundamentally tied to the practice of drawing. Mine are drawings that incorporate thread and wire, traditional painting materials, fabric and felt, walls, as well as paper and canvas." Lisa lives in the Bay Area with her husband and daughter and aging French Bulldog.

Me Adjust *by Lisa Solomon*

GET READY!

At the end of the year we often find ourselves reflecting back on the year. It's a great time to take photographs of family members and create a memory for years to come in stitches. This project can have more than one person in each hoop – that is up to the maker.

LET'S MAKE ART

1. Make sure your picture fits inside the embroidery hoop. Tape the photo to the underside of the muslin securely.

2. Hold the paper and muslin up to a window . Trace around the image with the pencil.

3. When finished tracing the face, features, shoulders and hair, remove the photo and place the muslin between the hoop. Secure the muslin tightly.

4. Thread the needle with the hair-colored floss. Make a knot at the end.

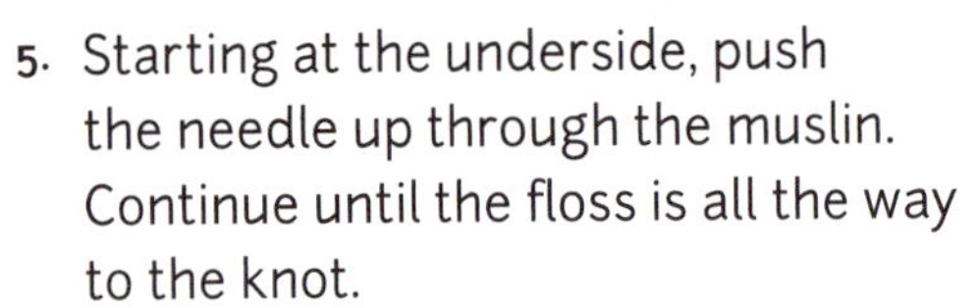

5. Starting at the underside, push the needle up through the muslin. Continue until the floss is all the way to the knot.

6. Using a running stitch push the needle back down through the muslin about one quarter inch or four mm away from the entry point, along the drawn line.

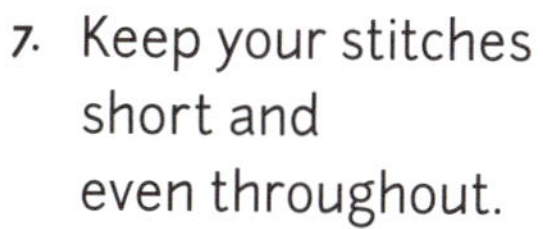

7. Keep your stitches short and even throughout.

8. Do not tie knots on the back of the work. Just leave them hanging about three inches.

9. Change colors for the different part of the portrait.

MATERIALS

- Journal
- Pencil
- Watercolors
- Water container
- Specimens to draw

INSPIRED BY SUSANN FOSTER BROWN

The acorns grew on a giant red oak tree next to our owner-built home in New Paltz, NY. I always loved the clusters of acorns and the promise of baby oak tress for future generations.

Red Oak *by Susann Foster Brown*

GET READY!

If the weather is nice enough, you can take this lesson outside to observe. It is also good to have your journal and a pencil on hand for a quick sketch when you are outside. You never know what you might want to draw!

LET'S MAKE ART!

1. Look over your specimens.
2. Choose one to draw.
3. Continue observing and adding details.
4. When you are finished drawing, go back and add watercolor as desired.
5. Keep adding each day to document your nature finds! Add a date to the page, too.

EXPLORE MORE

Keeping a visual journal is a wonderful way to have reminders of where you have been and how you saw things at a particular time. Use your sketches to create ideas for more artwork.

Fall Shadow Box

MATERIALS

- Small box with lid
- Glue stick
- Tacky Glue
- Acrylic paint
- Assorted colored and textural papers
- Markers

INSPIRED BY RACHEL BLUMBERG

Rachel Blumberg is a visual artist, musician, educator and filmmaker, who likes to play around with and combine different mediums and forms of expression to reveal human narratives, express emotions, re-explain historical events, and reveal hidden things. She especially loves using old found objects in all her work: film, music, and art alike.

Time Lapse *by Rachel Blumberg*

GET READY!

Many artists create art inside a container or box. Think first of what scene you would like to have inside your box. This lesson creates a landscape in three-dimensional form. Ask yourself these questions: What time of day or night is it? Where am I? Who or what can be seen?

LET'S MAKE ART!

1. Decide which way the box will open. Paint the outside of the box. We used a hinged cigar box.

2. Let dry and open to begin working on the inside. Use the box flap to create depth in the space.

3. Use cut and torn paper for the scene inside. You can make layers of smaller pieces of paper to add texture

4. Use a tab of paper to create standing objects.

5. Finish off details with markers.

EXPLORE MORE

There is no limit to what little worlds you can make inside of a box. Try creating the same landscape in different boxes at different times of the year.

Animal Forms

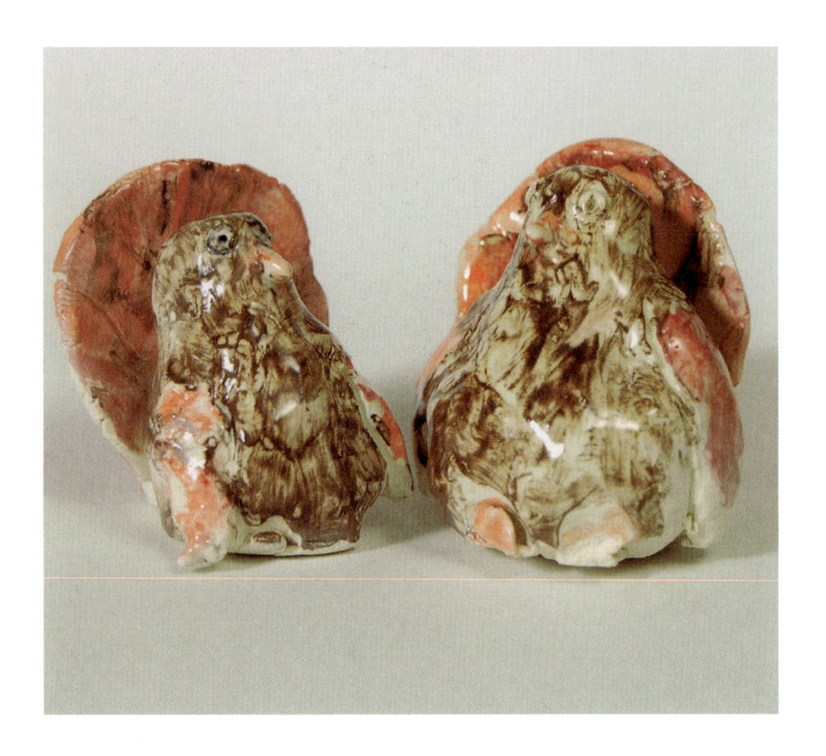

MATERIALS

- Low fire clay or oven-bake clay
- Glaze or acrylic paint
- Toothpick or skewer for details
- Water container
- Soft paintbrush

INSPIRED BY CAROL ROLL

I've always loved beautiful old, soft, faded and fragile things. I came up with the name Nostalgic Folk Art in 2004 when I started making my little imps, "toys" and primitive pieces because i wanted them to invoke those feelings I have when I see something that reminds me of a happy childhood.

The Hiker *by Carol Roll*

GET READY!

Animals are exciting to study and draw. They are even more fun to sculpt. Choose an animal you are interested in and study the details before beginning.

LET'S MAKE ART!

1. Start with a small ball of clay, the size of a large egg.
2. Form the basic shape of the body first.
3. Pull as many of the details of the animal out from the body as you can, instead of making them separately and attaching them on.
4. Smooth the cracks gently with your finger.
5. If you must add on pieces, make score lines as shown in the recipe section, if you are using low fire clay. For oven-bake clay smooth the joints thoroughly.
6. Fire or bake at the appropriate temperatures. Glaze with color and fire again, or paint with acrylics.

EXPLORE MORE

You can create a whole family of your favorite animals. Create a habitat for them, too!

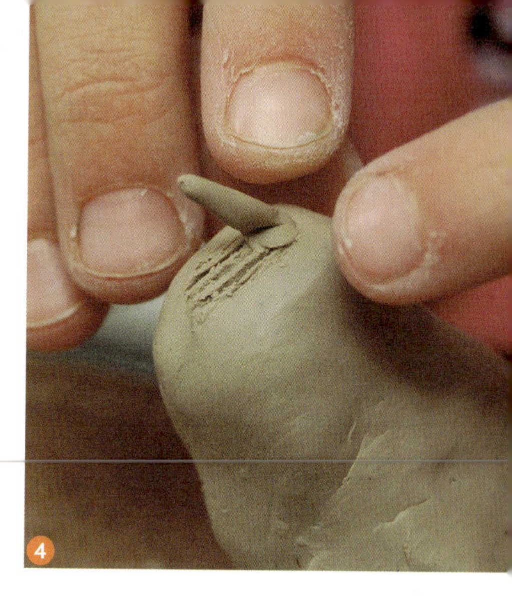

Printed Napkins

MATERIALS

- Cotton cloth napkins
- Apples
- Knife
- Textile block printing ink
- Newspaper
- Brayer
- Foam tray

EXPLORE MORE

Make a napkin for everyone in your family. Use their favorite color to print their napkin.

GET READY!

Printing on fabric is an addictive art form. Buy as many napkins for as there are guests at the table. Protect your printing space with plenty of newspaper!

INSPIRED BY JENNIFER HEWITT

Jen Hewett is a self-taught, San Francisco-based printmaker and surface designer. Working out of her tiny studio, Jen screenprints and block prints her bright, colorful work on fabric, and then sews it into bags and pillows. Her products have made their way to destinations all over the world.

Napkins by Jennifer Hewett

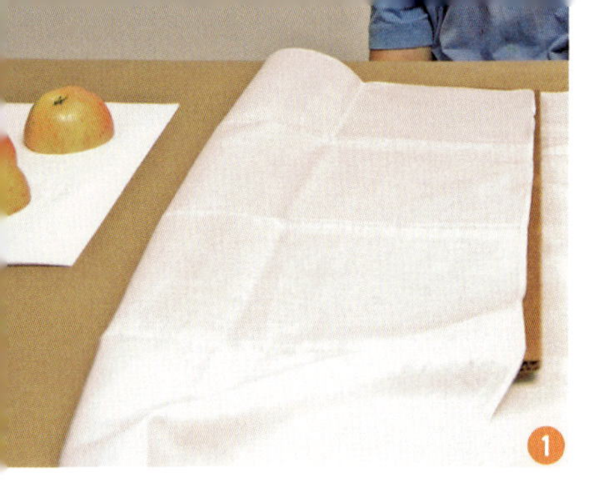

LET'S MAKE ART!

1. Have an adult cut two apples in half with a sharp knife. One should be cut from the top down to the bottom and one across the middle. Find the star!

2. We folded our napkin and pressed it gently to create twelve sections in which to print. It is one option for designing the composition. Think up more!

3. Roll out the ink with the brayer in the foam tray until smooth.

4. Roll the prepared ink onto the first apple. Coat it well.

5. Press the apple firmly on the napkin. Repeat with the second apple and make a pattern with them both until the napkin is complete.

6. If the apple is not printing fully, you could slip a small stack of newspaper under the napkin for a cushion. This will help create a crisper print. We liked the variations in each print. Let the ink dry and set the ink as directed on the label.

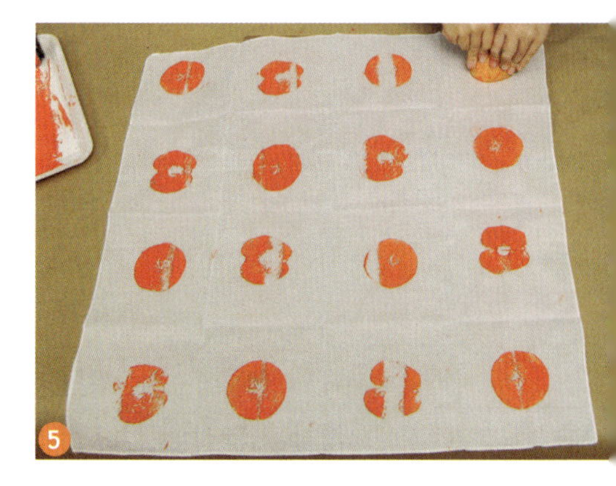

Leaf Table Runner

GET READY!

A table runner is a wonderful way to explore working with textiles as an art form. These are paintings for the table and can be of any design that you choose. We decided on leaves.

MATERIALS

- Burlap
- Assorted colored felt
- Assorted embroidery floss
- Embroidery needle
- Scissors
- Paper
- Pencil
- Tacky Glue

EXPLORE MORE

Why not make a table runner for each season of the year?

INSPIRED BY DAISY ADAMS ELLARD

Daisy Adams is a New Hampshire artist who works in a variety of mediums. When not pursuing her love of painting, she loves finding new ways to change sheets of felt into whimsical creations.

Felt Owl Banner by Daisy Adams Ellard

LET'S MAKE ART!

1. Cut a length of burlap half as long as the table you want to display it on. We used a burlap that was backed with plastic.
2. Draw a leaf shape on the paper. Draw a larger version and a smaller version too.
3. Cut them out. The paper leaves will become your pattern.
4. Lay the pattern on to the felt and trace around the leaf with a pencil.

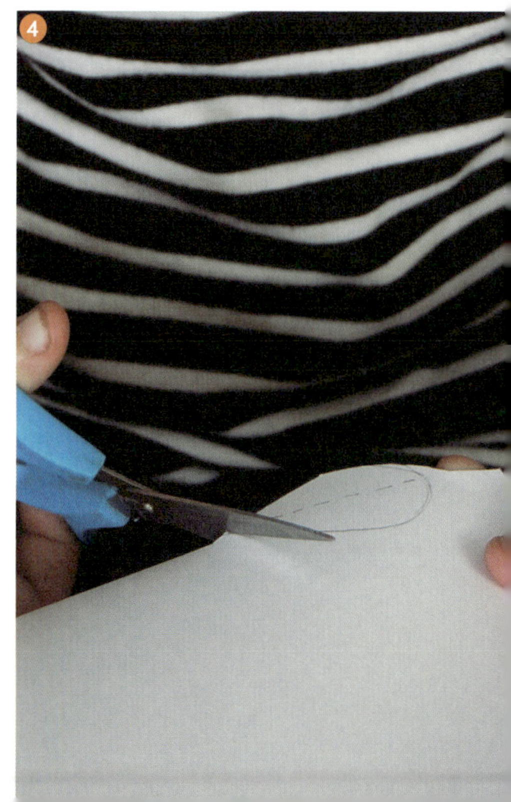

Leaf Table Runner

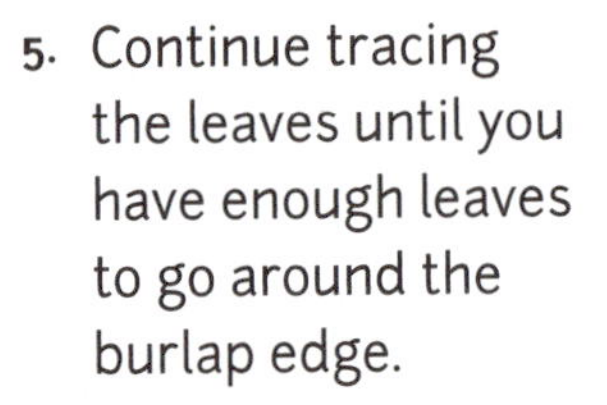

5. Continue tracing the leaves until you have enough leaves to go around the burlap edge.

6. Cut out the leaves and sort by color. Lay them out on the burlap as desired.

7. Embroider the center of each leaf with a contrasting thread. Use a simple running stitch and knot the end of the thread before you begin.

8. Tuck the loose threads under the leaves with a dot of glue. Lay the burlap on a piece of waxed paper to avoid glue on the table. Add more glue to the backside of the leaves and press firmly onto the burlap. Let dry and place on your table.

WINTER

WINTER

Painted windows of frost and pattern, snowflakes each unique and beautiful are simple pleasures of Winter. The land is sleepy with dark days and short bursts of sunlight. Long inky shadows of bare trees and fences are inspiring scenes to paint and draw from a warm window sill. The ever-changing landscape after a snowfall with soft sparkling mounds covering garden beds and porches are temporary, yet inviting to explore.

Tiny tracks circling around our yard create designs and patterns all their own from unknown animal artists. Giant icicles look like dragon's teeth hanging from every high ledge on a sunny winter's day. Taking a walk across an ice-covered lake or sliding down a smooth hill are experiences to bring back with you into the art studio. Skating on ice can be a paint-filled brush zooming over a canvas. Breathe in the stark beauty of winter and let it pour itself into your art.

MATERIALS

- Canvas or wood panel
- Tracing paper
- Acrylic paint
- Assorted brushes
- Water container
- Pencil
- Felt
- Clear glue

GET READY!

Lots of dogs wear sweaters in New England during our cold winters. Why not think up other animals that might like a sweater – or other item of clothing during the winter?

INSPIRED BY AMY RICE

I am as inspired in my art as much by childhood memories of growing up on a Midwestern farm as I am the urban community in which I now live. I am influenced by bicycles, street art, gardening, and random found objects, collective endeavors that challenge hierarchy, acts of compassion, downright silliness, and things with wings.

Woof by Amy Rice

LET'S MAKE ART!

1. With a pencil draw your animal wearing a sweater or other garment of your choice. Draw the area surrounding the animal.

2. Begin painting the background first.

3. Add the animal in with the acrylic paint, but leave the garment area blank. Let dry.

EXPLORE MORE

Your animals also could wear some nice boots. Try giving them scarves or hats!

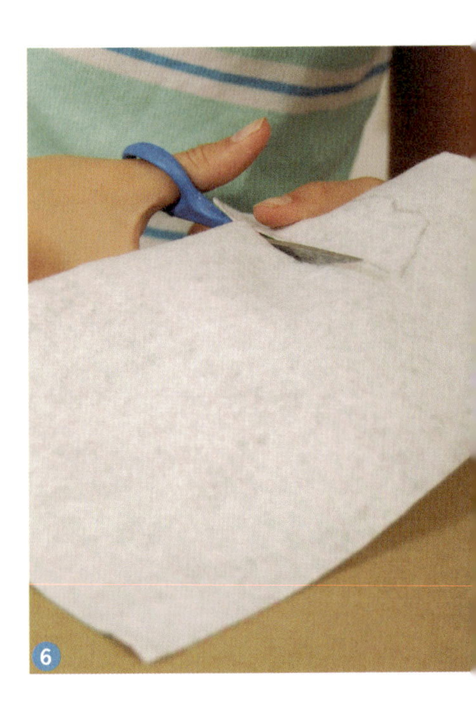

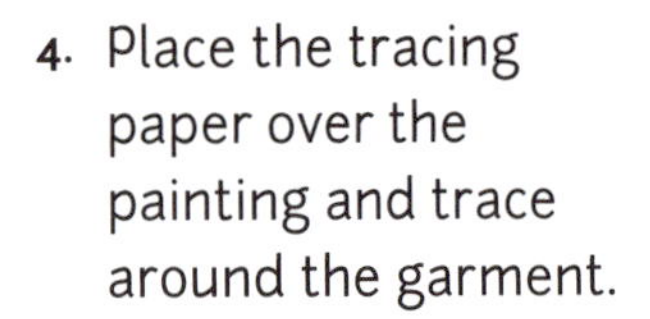

4. Place the tracing paper over the painting and trace around the garment.
5. Cut out the shape from the tracing paper. This will be your pattern.
6. Flip the pattern over and place on the back of the felt. Cut out the felt sweater.

7. Apply the glue to the board. Place the felt face down and press firmly to the board.

8. Use the paint pen for tiny details.

Salt Clay Ornaments

GET READY!

Tiny winter animals look so cute hanging from a bough or a doorknob. Salt clay is easy to make and easy to store for spontaneous sculptural projects. Have an adult help with the baking and the final clear coat spray!

MATERIALS

- Salt clay from recipe section
- Paper clip
- Wire cutters
- Watercolor pans
- Water container
- Toothpick or skewer
- Paintbrush
- Ribbon
- Clear coat spray (to be used outside by an adult)

EXPLORE MORE

There is no limit to what animals you can create with salt dough. Why not make an entire zoo filled with your favorite animals and hang them from a tree branch?

INSPIRED BY THE AUTHOR, SUSAN SCHWAKE

I have been making tiny animals as ornaments and as sculptures for over 30 years. I enjoy making tiny birds and creatures of my own design. These birds are my latest creations. One year I made two hundred tiny white doves – just to see if I could stick with it! Small can be beautiful.

Friends by Susan Schwake

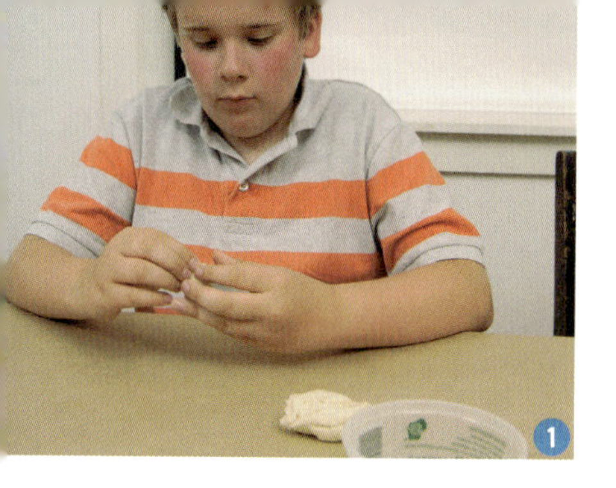

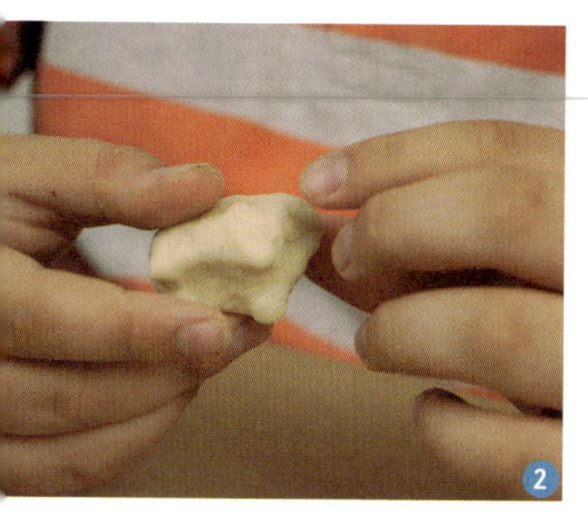

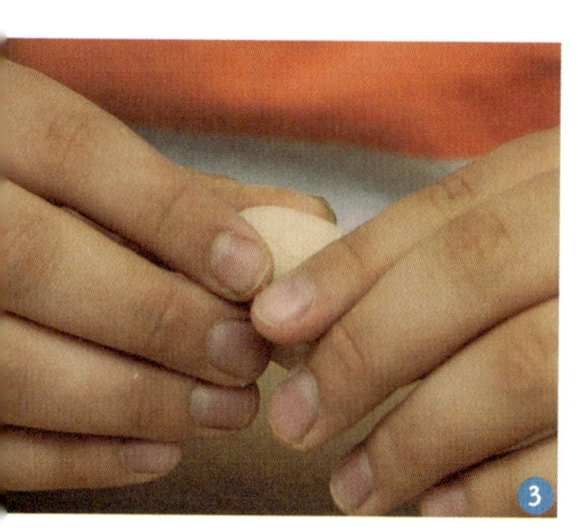

LET'S MAKE ART!

1. Start with a small ball of clay. Squeeze it in your hand to make sure it is smooth all over.

2. Pull the limbs, tail and head all from the rounded shape. Try not to add separate pieces, as they are more likely to fall off.

3. Using your finger, smooth any cracks that may have formed. If the animal is very thick, poke little holes in the clay with the toothpick. Also use the toothpick or skewer for adding details.

4. Cut a paper clip in half and stick the points down into the dough to create a hanger. Have an adult help with this step, if needed.

5. Let dry and bake at 350° F, until the ornament is hard. The time it takes to bake is dependent on how thick it is. Watch it carefully!

6. Let cool and paint as desired with watercolor paint.

7. Have an adult spray the ornament with a clear coat, outside. Tie with a ribbon to hang.

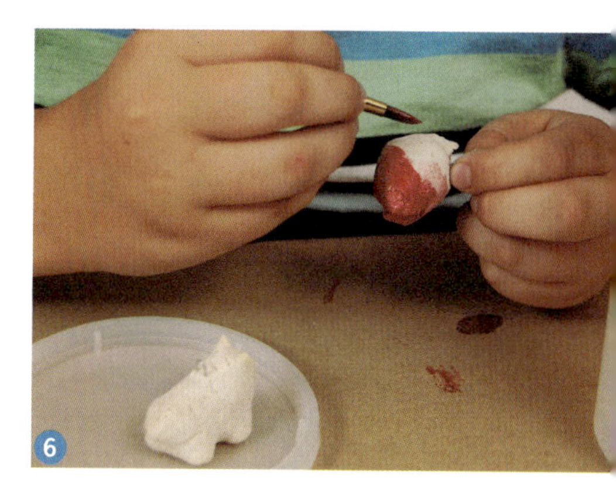

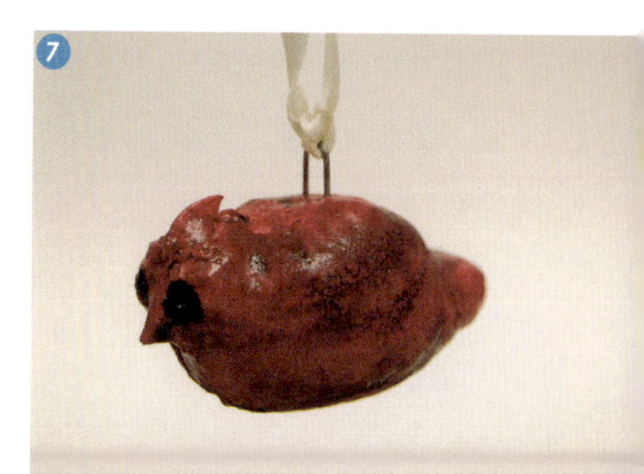

Snowy Prints

MATERIALS

- Pencil with a new eraser
- Plastic lids
- Black paint
- White paint
- Colored paper
- Potato
- Brayer

INSPIRED BY JOHN TERRY DOWNS

Terry Downs is a professional printmaker and retired professor of art from Plymouth State University in New Hampshire. He was also this author's mentor. His love of printmaking is infectious and his work inspiring. This print was created with relief and intaglio methods.

The Maternal Bond *by Terry Downs*

GET READY!

A snowy day brings grey skies and lots of snowflakes. Printmaking is the perfect medium to reproduce these conditions on paper! Have an adult cut the potato in half with a sharp knife.

LET'S MAKE ART!

1. Dispense a small amount of white acrylic paint in the plastic lid. Dip the eraser from the pencil into it.

2. Press and turn the paint-filled eraser on the paper to create the snowflakes. Continue until you are satisfied with your "snowstorm."

3. With a sharpened pencil, carve a snowflake into the potato half.

4. Make sure the lines are deep by going over them two or three times.

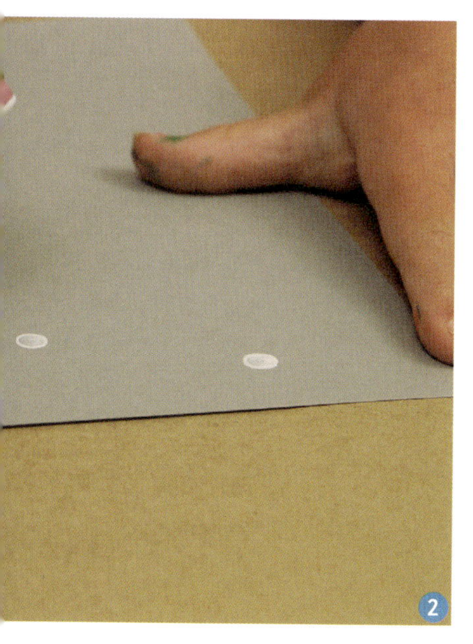

EXPLORE MORE

You can print a snowflake with a potato and textile ink onto a dark colored tee shirt. A stack of newspapers inside the shirt keeps the paint from leaking through to the back.

Snowy Prints

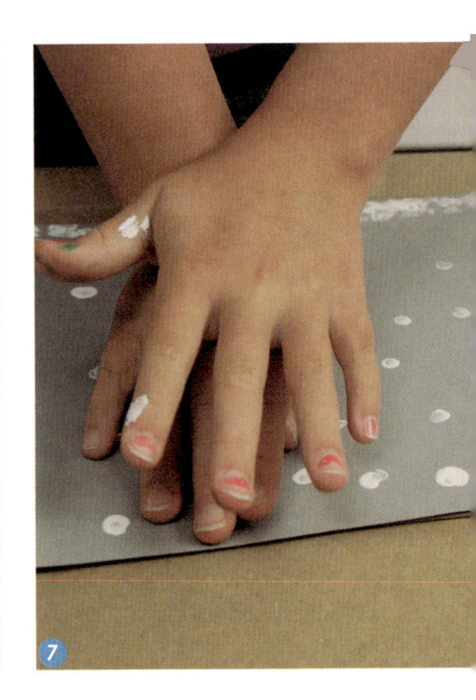

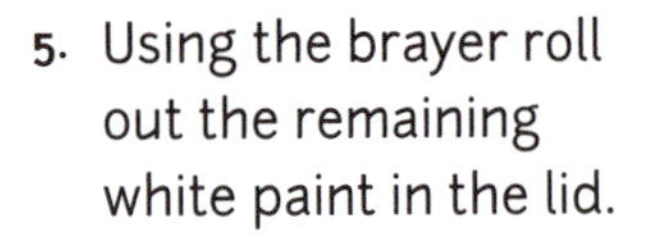

5. Using the brayer roll out the remaining white paint in the lid.

6. Roll the paint onto the potato evenly.

7. Print the snowflake potato onto your paper by pressing firmly on the potato.

8. Lift up the potato to expose your print.
9. Continue printing snowflakes as desired. You can print them partially off the paper to show movement.
10. Dispense some black paint into another plastic lid. Dip the pencil eraser into the paint.
11. Using the eraser create some bare trees amongst the snowflakes.

Mini Art Accordion Books

MATERIALS

- Heavy sketching paper twice as long as it is wide
- Watercolor paper
- Card stock
- Colored pencils
- Watercolor pans
- Water container
- Glue stick
- Soft brush
- Mat board
- Newspaper
- Pencils

EXPLORE MORE

These little books can be fictional or non-fiction. Make one for each memorable event from each season of the year!

INSPIRED BY DARRYL JOEL BERGER

Darryl Joel Berger is the author of two collections of short stories – Punishing Ugly Children and Dark All Day. His fiction and illustrations have appeared in many magazines. With his wife Christina, he runs a literary press called Upstart Press in Kingston, Ontario.

Mini accordion books by DJ Berger

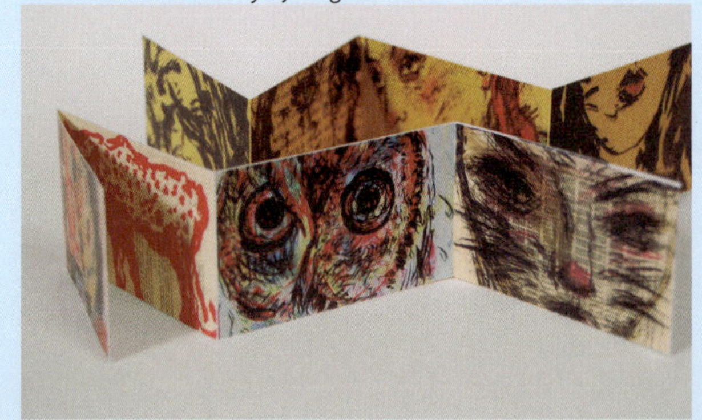

GET READY!

Think first about how you are going to tell a story without words. Each drawing in the book will tell a piece of the story. Ours is about Winter. Get your ideas together by sketching them out on a paper first, or simply make a list of your ideas.

LET'S MAKE ART!

1. Begin by cutting a long piece of paper and folding it accordion style. Start by folding it in half. Then fold those halves in half.

2. Cut two pieces of mat board slightly larger than the folded book. These will be the backing for the covers.

3. Cut the watercolor paper slightly larger than the mat board covers.

4. Cut card stock into pieces slightly smaller than each page in the book. Cut one for each page.

5. Draw your story on the card stock pieces using pencil and colored pencil.

6

7

6. Glue each story card onto the accordion pages. Continue on the backside pages, too, if desired.
7. Draw out your covers both front and back onto the watercolor papers. Add watercolor to the covers and let dry.
8. Glue the watercolor covers to the mat boards.
9. Glue the accordion pages to the mat board covers.
10. Stand your book up for display!

8

10

Paper Trees

GET READY!

These little trees are a fun way to recall winter walks in the snowy woods. They are fun to make and a great way to use up discarded books or sheet music. We kept ours the color of the paper but you could paint them with transparent watercolor for a different effect.

MATERIALS

- Old book pages
- Sheet music
- Glue stick
- Ruler
- Pencil
- Brown paper
- White paper
- Heavy weight paper for background
- Scissors
- Circular object to trace – a CD is a good size!

INSPIRED BY LISA CONGDON

Lisa Congdon is a mixed media artist and illustrator from Oakland, California. She illustrates for such clients as *Martha Stewart Living* and *The Museum of Modern Art*, among others. She is the author of *Whatever You Are, Be a Good One*, and *Art Inc*. Much of her work is inspired by both nature and folk pattern. This particular piece, called *Folk Forest*, was inspired by a grove of trees she saw while riding her bike through Northern California – and combines her love of both trees and pattern.

Folk Forest *by Lisa Congdon*

LET'S MAKE ART!

1. Trace the circle onto the book page or sheet music with a pencil. Cut out the circle.

2. Using the ruler draw a line through the middle of the circle and cut the circle in half.

3. First fold from the straight edge at the bottom to more than half the way up the straight side. Experiment with the shape of the first wedge to create skinny or plump trees!

4. Flip over the half circle and fold it again to the same end point. The folds should slightly extend over the previous ones.

5. Continue folding in this manner until the paper is all folded.

6. Glue down the last fold.

EXPLORE MORE

Add details to your collage with drawing tiny birds in the trees or some tracks in the snow!

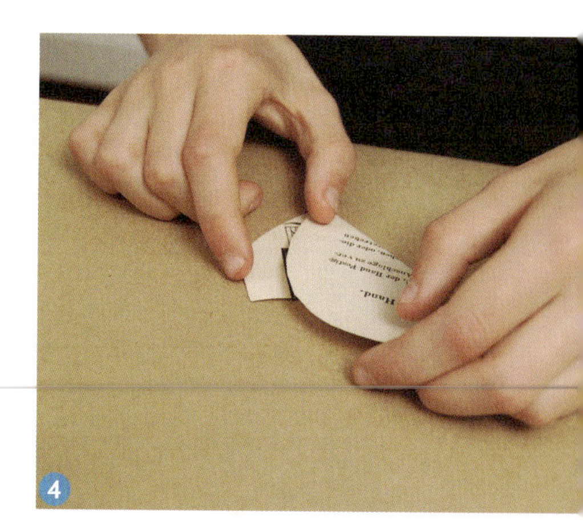

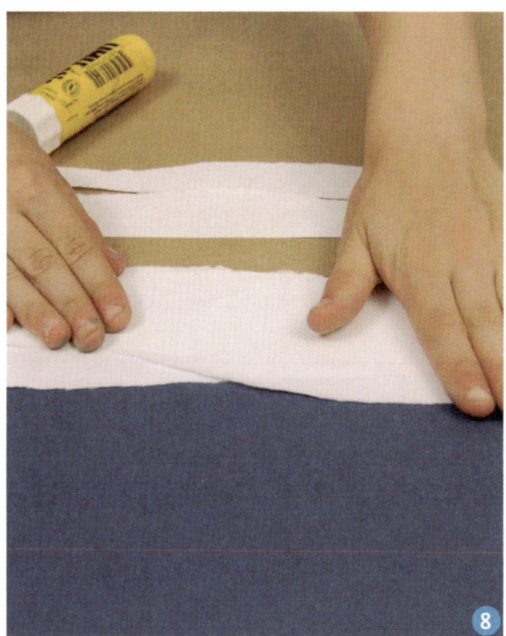

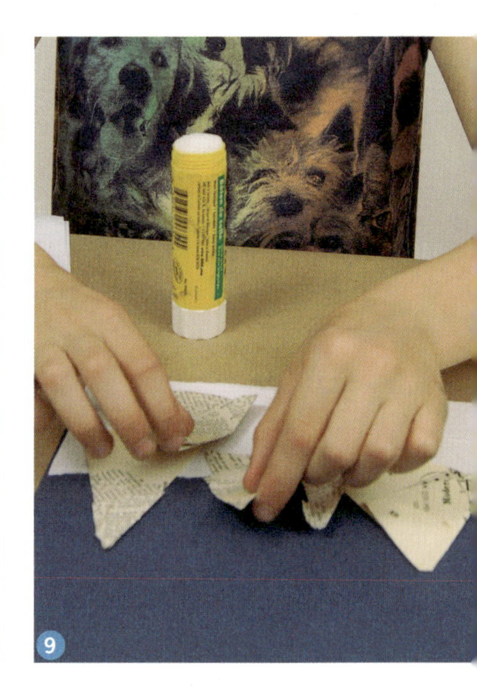

7. Tear some of the white paper into strips for the snowy ground.

8. Glue the ground paper to the heavyweight background paper.

9. Glue the trees to the snowy ground.

10. Glue the brown paper trunks to the trees.

11. You can add a moon or clouds or snowflakes to complete your collage.

MATERIALS

- Assorted colored papers
- Glue stick
- Washi tape
- Card stock
- Ruler
- Pencil

GET READY!

Winter at our home includes warm quilts on the beds. Quilts can be created from scraps of colorful fabric –so why not try a beautiful paper scrap quilt with your leftover artwork? Any paper will work for this as long as it appeals to you. Study a book of quilts from your local library to gather ideas for your quilt pattern or make one up!

INSPIRED BY CILLA STILES

This tapestry was pieced together from upholstery samples. The vertical lines represent both tree trunks and beams of sunlight as they filter through the forest canopy. And of course there is a snake in every Eden, representing that which is both seductively beautiful and threatening.

Tapestry by Cilla Stiles, photo Phil Stiles

LET'S MAKE ART!

1. Cut a small square from the card stock as a pattern for the blocks that you will make your quilt from.
2. Using a pencil and your square pattern, trace around the square on the backside of the papers you have chosen.
3. Continue until you have all the squares you need for your paper quilt.
4. Cut some of the papers diagonally in half to make triangles, if desired. Use a ruler to make straight lines.

EXPLORE MORE

Look for a quilt show in your town or visit a museum to view actual quilts. Choose a traditional pattern and try making a paper version of your own.

Paper Quilts

5. Arrange your squares and triangles on another piece of card stock in the pattern you choose.

6. When arranged, begin gluing the pieces down to the card stock.

7. Finish gluing all the squares and rectangles down on the card stock.

8. Use the washi tape to create a border all around the edges of the quilt.

Winter Animal Banner

GET READY!

Celebrate the animal kingdom with a sweet little banner! Choose your favorite animals that romp in the wintertime.

MATERIALS

- Card stock
- Oil pastels with the paper stripped off
- Scissors
- Watercolor pans
- Soft brush
- Water container
- Newspaper
- Texture plates
- Seam binding
- Glue stick
- Tacky Glue

EXPLORE MORE

Make your banner twice as much fun with an animal on both sides. You can hang it in a doorway to view both sides.

INSPIRED BY BLAIR STOCKER

Blair Stocker is author of *Wise Craft: Turning Thrift Store Finds, Fabric Scraps, and Natural Objects into Stuff You Love.* A quilter, artist, and avid DIYer, Blair lives in Seattle, WA with her husband, two kids, and a fat kitty named Gracie.

Gathering Bunting *by Blair Stocker*

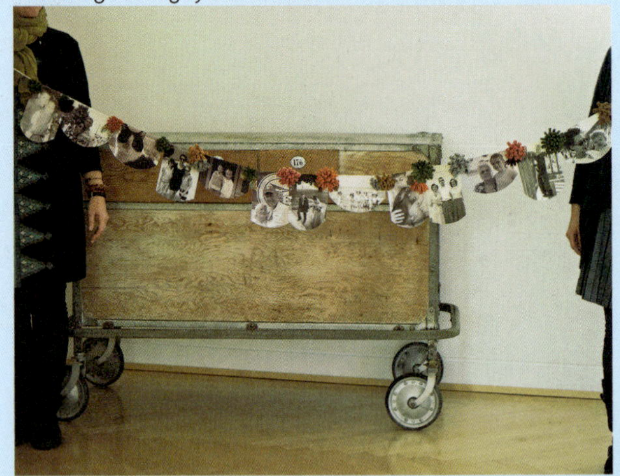

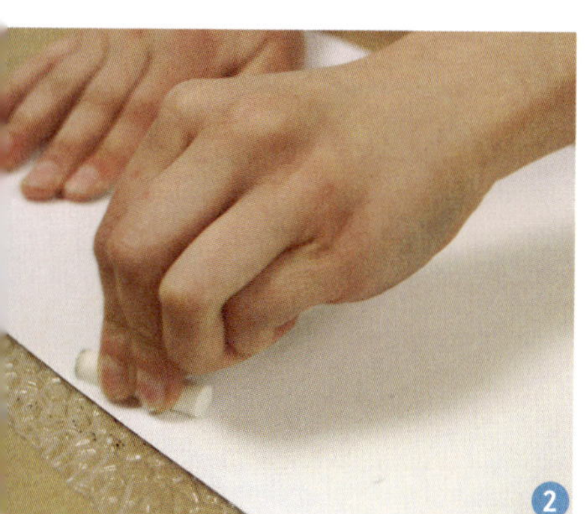

LET'S MAKE ART!

1. Sketch out the animals first to decide which animals you want to include in your banner.

2. Place the texture plate under a piece of card stock, rub a white or light-colored oil pastel over the card stock creating visual texture. Continue until the paper is covered. Make two pieces of card stock in this fashion.

3. Paint over the texture with watercolor using a color that is darker than the oil pastel. Let dry.

4. Trace around the banner flag template from the recipe section (page 140) and cut out a flag from the textured paper for each animal.

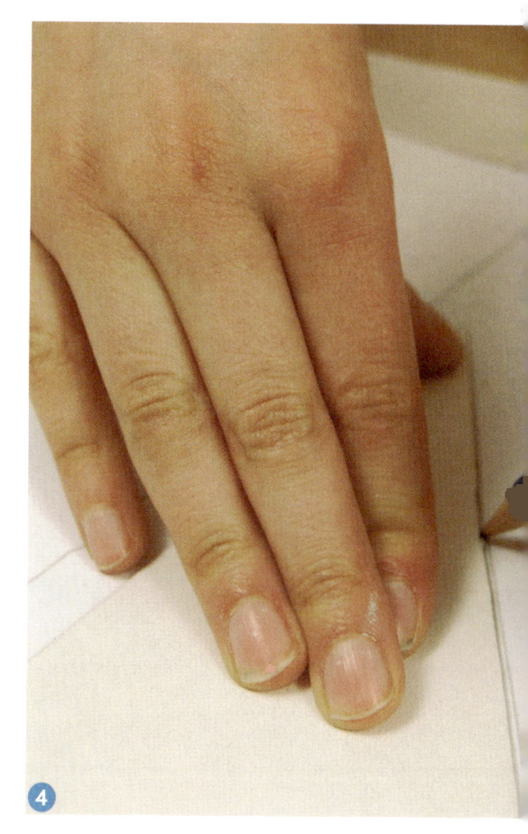

5. Using a sheet of card stock, cut out a circle from the template in the recipe section for each animal you have chosen. Use pinking shears if you want a fancy edge on your circle.

6. Draw your animal with pencil first and then add color with oil pastel.

7. Glue your circles with the animals onto the flags.

8. Lay out your flags in the order desired. Squeeze the Tacky Glue on the back top edge of your flag. Place the flags on seam binding and press firmly to seal. Let dry.

9. Hang up your banner on the wall!

Tin Can Tracks

GET READY!

Visit your local library to find a book on animal tracks. Choose a few to draw. Each animal has a distinctive track that it makes in the mud or snow.

MATERIALS

- Tin can (soup-sized can)
- Self-adhesive foam sheets
- Ink pads
- Ballpoint pen
- Ruler
- Animal track reference book

EXPLORE MORE

This method of printing is exciting and can be used to print large sheets of paper for wrapping paper or murals. Try to go big with your paper size!

INSPIRED BY THE NATIONAL AUDUBON SOCIETY

I enjoy bird watching and watching animals when I can find them! The National Audubon Society has sparked my enthusiasm for finding animal tracks with their guides. Check out their books from your local library and explore nature.

LET'S MAKE ART!

1. Draw the outline of each track, left and right for each animal on the craft foam.

2. Cut out the shapes of the tracks.

3. Cover the tin can with a sheet of craft foam, trimmed to size.

4. Take the paper backing off the animal tracks you cut out and stick them on top of the sheet of craft foam on the can. Line up the right and left and back and front tracks.

5. Continue this all around the can.

6. Press an ink pad onto the tracks – make sure to press firmly.

7. Starting at one end of the paper, roll the inked tracks over the paper. Continue until your paper is filled with animal tracks!

Forest Plaster Cottage

MATERIALS

- Plaster
- Small paper cups
- Water
- Container for mixing plaster
- Wooden craft stick
- Toothpick
- Tissue
- Mod Podge
- Watercolor pans
- Water container
- Soft brush
- Newspaper

EXPLORE MORE

These little cottages can be used as winter decorations with tiny clay animals or a collection of found objects from your nature adventures. Create a whole village of cottages.

GET READY!

Plaster is easy to carve. Make sure an adult helps you measure and mix the plaster. Always remember to let the remaining plaster harden to dispose of it. Never pour plaster down a drain.

INSPIRED BY THE WIND IN THE WILLOWS

The book "The Wind in the Willows" by Kenneth Grahame celebrates nature and the passing of seasons beautifully. The animal characters are delightful and some of them lived in homes I like to imagine, similar to these cottages. The book truly inspired me to create this lesson!

Always inspiring, New Hampshire artist Megan Bogonovich created this tiny clay house. www.meganbogonovich.com

LET'S MAKE ART!

1. Mix the plaster according to directions and pour into small paper cups.

2. When the plaster is hard, tear off the paper cup.

3. Rub and carve the plaster on top of a newspaper to create the shape of the roof.

4. Use a bristle brush to remove plaster from the carved lines.

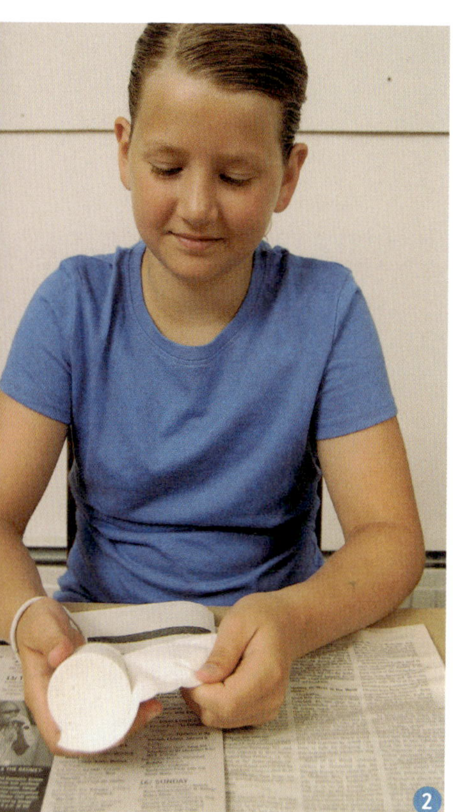

Forest Plaster Cottage

5. Use a toothpick to carve designs into the sides of the house.

6. Create a door, windows, chimney and other details as desired.

7. Add color with watercolor paints.

8. Rub with a tissue to force the color into the lines you have drawn.

9. Use as many colors as you like.

9. Seal your cottages with Mod Podge.

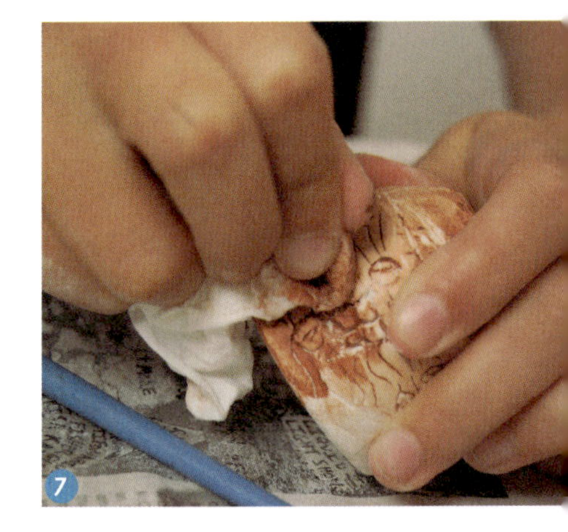

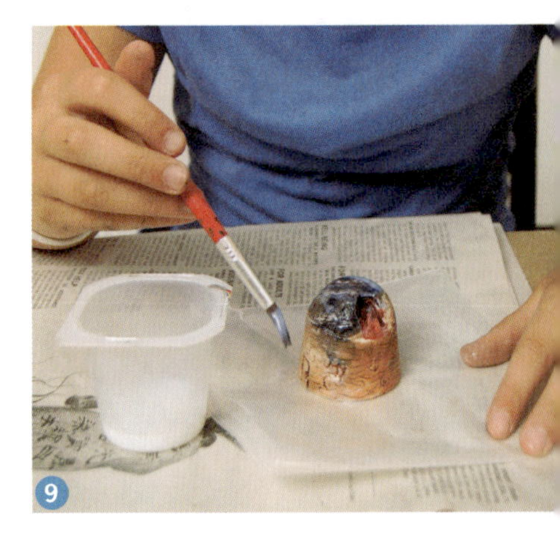

Winter Night Drawing

MATERIALS

- Assorted gel pens
- Pencil
- White drawing paper
- Black drawing paper

INSPIRED BY SUSANNA GORDON

Susanna Gordon studied art and photography at the Ontario College of Art & Design in Toronto. She began blogging in 2006 and has found an entirely new, wonderful world full of creative individuals.

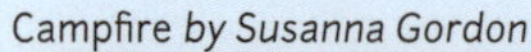

Campfire *by Susanna Gordon*

GET READY!

Nighttime drawings or paintings are always dramatic. There is a bit of mystery about the night and it's fun to try and capture that in a drawing. Think first about what creatures sleep or hibernate during the winter. And also who's awake in the forest at night!

LET'S MAKE ART!

1. Using a pencil and white sketch paper, decide what your composition will be.

2. Once you have decided, use the gel pens to draw your picture onto the black paper.

3. Remember to make lots of details in your drawing to show texture of the animals and objects.

4. Remember to show the weather conditions in your nighttime drawing. Are there clouds or a moon? Is it snowing or windy?

5. Show what the animals are doing in your drawing. Are they awake or asleep?

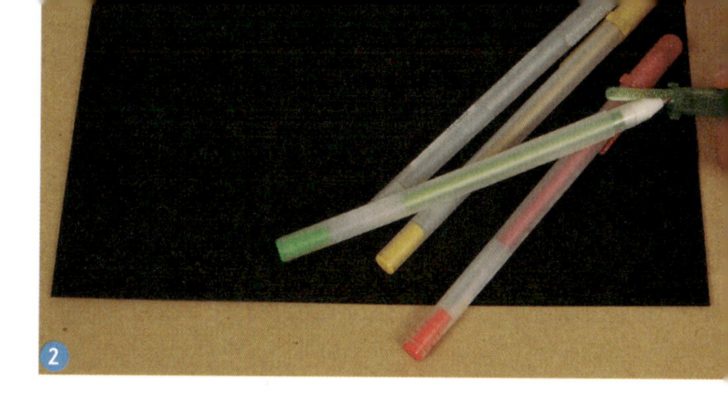

2

3

5

EXPLORE MORE

A good book to read before this lesson is "Owl Moon" by Jane Yolen and John Schoenherr. Its beautiful nighttime illustrations will get everyone in the mood for drawing a night scene.

SETTING UP A PAINTING AREA

Place a folded sheet of newspaper on the right side of your paper if you are right handed and on the left if you are left handed. This is where you put your water container, brushes, and your Plexiglas paint palette. An extra piece folded in half again is good for wiping off water or excess paint. Set it up this way and you will avoid most accidents. Have your scrap piece of white paper slipped under the palette for testing colors. Setting up your workspace is a ritual that makes creating much easier. With acrylic paints, dispense coin sized amounts, add retarder to slow down the drying time, and mix with palette knives for easy clean up.

PAPIER-MÂCHÉ GOO:

Sprinkle a handful of flour or two into a bowl of warm water. Stir until mixed. Add more flour until the mixture becomes the consistency of cream.

Use small strips or rectangles of newspaper that have been torn with the grain of the paper. The grain of the paper tears easily – across the grain does not.

SALT CLAY

- 1-½ cup of salt
- 1-½ cup of hot water
- 4 cups flour (up to)

Dump salt and hot water into a bowl and stir until salt dissolves. Add flour until mixture becomes gummy- up to four cups. Knead it for 10 minutes until smooth. Will keep in the refrigerator for months but warm to room temperature before using.

WORKING WITH SALT CLAY TIPS

- Glue together pieces with water.
- Let dry 7–10 hours before baking.
- Bake at 300˚ F for 1-½–2 hours for ½ inch thick pieces
- Prick the piece all over with a toothpick or sewing needle to avoid bubbles

SETTING UP FOR WORKING WITH CLAY

For working with clay you will need a wooden surface or a sheet of canvas to roll and work the clay on. A small dish of water and a scoring tool are basic items to have on hand. Texture can be made by simple household items such as lace, cardboard, buttons, earrings, old flatware, screens, woven items, anything that you can feel texture can be printed into clay for actual texture.

ROLLING A SLAB OF CLAY

For making slabs of clay, you will need a rolling pin or fat dowel to roll the clay out. Using two slats of wood on either side of the clay will keep the slab an even thickness. At our studio, we make slabs as follows:

- Start with a wedged slab of clay. Lay your wood strips to either side of the clay with the rolling pin touching both sides
- Start in the middle of the clay with your hands close to the middle on top of the pin.
- Roll back and forth—only in the middle—three or four times and then flip. You don't have to press very hard.
- Continue until the clay is the thickness of the slats. Don't worry about the ends; they will flatten out as you flip.

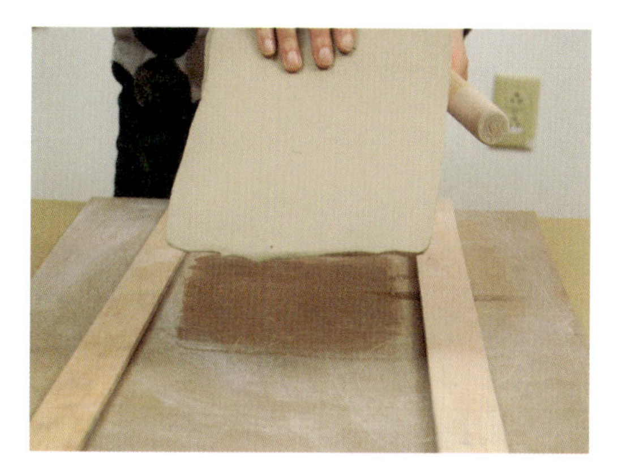

SCORING CLAY TO STICK TWO PIECES TOGETHER

Scrape both pieces of clay where you want to join them together. Dip the tool into the water and scrape one way and then another to make the area really rough. Press together firmly! Blend away the edges of the lines with your finger to smooth.

Templates for Animal Banner (page 126)

Resources

AUSTRALIA

Eckersley's Arts, Crafts, and Imagination
www.eckersleys.com.au

CANADA

Curry's Art Store
Ontario, Canada
www.currys.com

DeSerres
www.deserres.ca

Michaels
www.michaels.com

Opus Framing & Art Supplies
www.opusframing.com

FRANCE

Graphigro
Paris, France
www.graphigro-paris11.fr

ITALY

Vertecchi
Rome, Italy
www.vertecchi.com

NEW ZEALAND

Littlejohns Art & Graphic Supplies Ltd.
Wellington, New Zealand

UNITED KINGDOM

T N Lawrence & Son Ltd.
www.lawrence.co.uk

Creative Crafts
www.creativecrafts.co.uk

UNITED STATES

A. C. Moore
www.acmoore.com

Baily Pottery Supply
www.bailypottery.com

Big Ceramic Store
www.bigceramicstore.com

Daniel Smith
www.danielsmith.com

Dick Blick
www.dickblick.com

Jo-Ann Fabric and Craft Stores
www.joann.com

Michaels
www.michaels.com

Sheffield Pottery Supply
www.sheffield-pottery.com

Utrecht
www.utrechtart.com

Contributors

THANK YOU TO ALL THE ARTISTS

ALBINA MCPHAIL
www.albinamcphail.com

HEATHER SMITH JONES
www.heathersmithjones.com

JENNIFER SKOROPOWSKI
www.jenskistudio.blogspot.com

BRIDGETTE GUERZON MILLS
www.guerzonmills.com

JENNIFER HEWETT
www.jenhewett.com

ANDREA KULISH
andrikaspysanky.wordpress.com

CILLA STILES
www.nattyflies.etsy.com

MEGAN BOGONOVICH
www.meganbogonovich.com

ADAM PEARSON
www.pearsonsculpture.com.

CADA DRISCOLL
www.cadacreates.blogspot.com

JUDITH HELLER CASSELL
Rochester, NH

ASHLEY GOLDBERG
www.etsy.com/shop/ashleyg

CHRISTOPHER VOLPE
www.christophervolpe.com

LISA CONGDON
www.lisacongdon.com

JEANNÉ MCCARTIN
Portsmouth NH

LISA SOLOMON
www.lisasolomon.com

SUSANN FOSTER BROWN
www.cellarbrookfarm.com

RACHEL BLUMBERG
www.rachelblumberg.com

CAROL ROLL
nostalgicfolkart.blogspot.com

DAISY ADAMS ELLARD
www.etsy.com/shop/LucysArtEmporium

AMY RICE
www.amyrice.com

JOHN TERRY DOWNS
jupiter.plymouth.edu/~tdowns/

DARRYL JOEL BERGER
www.cigartinstories.wordpress.com

BLAIR STOCKER
www.wisecrafthandmade.com

SUSANNA GORDON
www.susannassketchbook.typepad.com

Addison, Andrew, Arianna, August, Ethan, Graham, Greta, Harper, Noa, Riley, Ruby & Ruby – Thank you!

About the Author

Susan Schwake is an artist, art educator, author and curator. Her passion for teaching art for over 20 years has found her working in diverse settings such as private and public schools, community organizations, programs for medically fragile children, special needs agencies, summer camps, intergenerational facilities, libraries, and her own little art school to thousands of people. Most recently she has taken her classroom online. Rainer Schwake produced the new series of e-courses called: *Art Class* including courses in Painting, Mixed Media, Printmaking and Hand-building with Clay.

Susan was hired to organize and create a permanent exhibition of children's art, involving more than one hundred local children. The children created the artwork for a new children's wing in the local library. She also directed a similar project with four hundred people in an intergenerational setting for a new multi-agency facility. This program was designed to bring the staff, families, and clients more closely together through the process of making art together and the artwork is permanently displayed in the facility.

Following the release of her first three books of the *Art Lab for Kids* series Susan continues to offer workshops and programs to parents, teachers at universities, art studios, community organization, public and private schools.

She exhibits her own artwork in galleries in the United States and Europe. Susan has been juried public art exhibitions, creating large-scale, site-specific outdoor works. To date, she has curated over 100 compelling contemporary exhibitions in her own gallery with of hundreds of national and international artists' work. She worked with many corporations installing original artwork from her gallery's stable of artists.

Susan works alongside her husband Rainer at artstream studios in New Hampshire. Together they collaborate daily within each facet of their creative business. Rainer holds a masters degree in Graphic Design from FH Münster, Germany, and has created award winning websites and print materials for companies in a wide range of sectors. Art for All Seasons features Rainer's layout and design, including over 400 photographs that the couple styled together and photographed. They work together creating exhibit layouts, media design work and promoting the art school, which they have built together. They wouldn't have it any other way. They have two creative children who write and make art and delight them endlessly.

Website: www.susanschwake.com
Gallery: www.artstreamstudios.com
Blog: www.artesprit.blogspot.com